D0729741

PENGUIN BOOKS

GROW UP

Ben Brooks was born in 1992 and lives in Gloucestershire, England. He is also the author of the novels *Fences*, *An Island of Fifty* and *The Kasahara School of Nihilism*. Brooks's work has been nominated for a Pushcart Prize and published in the Dzanc Books "Best of the Web" anthology.

GROW UP

BEN BROOKS

PENGUIN BOOKS

PENGUIN BOOKS
Published by the Penguin Group
Penguin Group (USA) Inc., 375 Hudson Street, New York, New York 10014, USA
Penguin Group (Canada), 90 Eglinton Avenue East, Suite 700, Toronto,
Ontario, Canada M4P 2Y3 (a division of Pearson Penguin Canada Inc.)
Penguin Books Ltd, 80 Strand, London WC2R 0RL, England
Penguin Ireland, 25 St Stephen's Green, Dublin 2, Ireland (a division of Penguin Books Ltd)
Penguin Group (Australia), 250 Camberwell Road, Camberwell,
Victoria 3124, Australia (a division of Pearson Australia Group Pty Ltd)
Penguin Books India Pvt Ltd, 11 Community Centre,
Panchsheel Park, New Delhi – 110 017, India
Penguin Group (NZ), 67 Apollo Drive, Rosedale, Auckland 0632,
New Zealand (a division of Pearson New Zealand Ltd)
Penguin Books (South Africa) (Pty) Ltd, 24 Sturdee Avenue,
Rosebank, Johannesburg 2196, South Africa

Penguin Books Ltd, Registered Offices: 80 Strand, London WC2R 0RL, England

First published in Great Britain by Canongate Books Ltd. 2011
Published in Penguin Books 2012

1 3 5 7 9 10 8 6 4 2

LIBRARY OF CONGRESS CATALOGING-IN-PUBLICATION DATA
Brooks, Ben, 1992–
Grow up / Ben Brooks.
p. cm.
ISBN 978-0-14-312109-1
1. Teenage boys—England—Fiction. I. Title.
PR6102.R6626G76 2012
823'.92—dc23 2011042962

Printed in the United States of America

Oh, WE KID OURSELVES THERE'S FUTURE
IN THE FUCKING, BUT THERE IS NO
FUCKING FUTURE

—"We Are Beautiful, We Are Doomed,"
Los Campesinos!

GROW UP

PART 1

Red Sex and Small Deaths

1

It is 2:46 a.m. and I am not asleep. Insomnia can result from an overactive thyroid gland, diabetes, violent muscle twitching, eating a heavy meal or excessive caffeine consumption. It can also result from stress. I am stressed because I am thinking of Keith and how he murdered his ex-wife.

I go to www.girlsoncam.com, enter my nickname as "Mr. Hard" and click "enter room."

You: hey
Sexythai: hi babe, feelin horny?

Sexythai is short and very thin. Her skin is the color of weak tea and her olive eyes are disproportionately wide. She is lying on a moth-eaten chaise longue that quivers as her pelvis gyrates.

You: sure

Sexythai: wanna go private?

Private is where you pay money to see the girl just you and her, and you can tell her to finger herself or repeatedly shout your name or pretend to be your art teacher. I do not pay to go private with girls. If you are tactful you can sometimes elicit nipple-flashes or quick glimpses of clit from them without paying anything.

Sexythai: baby?

Pause.

Sexythai is using her hands to draw my attention to her crotch. She is selling herself to me because, despite rapid industrialization, Thailand remains a poverty-stricken country.

I don't know what I am doing.

I am bored.

I am a large, empty grain silo.

You: are you a Buddhist?

She definitely is. Ninety-five percent of all Thais are Buddhist.

Sexythai: yes

I knew it.

You: Theravada?

Pause.

Sexythai: yes, private babe
You: i could just look this up on Wikipedia.

Pause.

Sexythai: look this

She pulls a decidedly un-erect nipple from its bra cup and begins to squeeze the teat in my direction. I feel vaguely intimidated but willing to continue.

You: what is your name?

Pause.

Sexythai: i want you in me baby
You: don't say that, don't ruin the mood
Sexythai: come in private
You: I like it here, it's less expensive

Pause.

You: how many baht to the pound?

She logs off.

I write down “Mr. Hard” and “Sexythai” on a piece of paper because I feel as though we have developed a “special connection” and I would like to talk with her again one evening. Perhaps I will rescue her from poverty in Thailand and we will marry. I bookmark the “oriental” category as a favorite. You should not have favorites. Dad was my favorite.

Keith is a murderer.

Dad was not.

2

Morning. 8:35 a.m. I am stood at my window looking into the garden. Keith is in the garden massaging the soil. He is probably imagining that the soil is the cleavage of a human cadaver. He is probably going to rub his face in the soil.

Above him the sky is stratified like Neapolitan ice cream. Salmon. Amber. Sepia. They fall and fade into each other. Salmoanmbesrepia. It smells of beer and tobacco and paper in my room. The glass smells of dust and old, trapped sun. Birds are flirting in the clouds.

I turn on my laptop and log on to Facebook. It says that Georgia Treely is online on Facebook chat. Georgia Treely probably isn't online on Facebook chat. Facebook chat is tricking me.

Georgia Treely is in my Psychology class. I want to

have a sexual relationship with Georgia Treely but I can't because she believes in Jesus and her mum shops at Waitrose. The best I can hope for is teenage rebellion against the values of her home environment. If ever this happens I will offer myself up as a medium for revolt. When my penis enters her vagina she will be thinking of how much she hates her mum and how unreasonable her curfews are.

I have never spoken to Georgia Treely.

I open a chat window.

Me: hello
Me: hello
Me: hello
Me: hello
Me: sorry
Me: hello
Me: hello
Me: you aren't there
Me: will you still read this
Me: maybe not
Me: no
Me: hello
Me: okay
Me: sh

Georgia Treely is offline.

I close the laptop and pick some clothes off the floor. Keith strokes weeds in the garden. It is almost time to meet Tenaya.

+

I am certain that Keith is a murderer. If you look at his history close enough, you can see that his ex-wife seems to just disappear, benefiting him in the process. Margaret Clamwell. May she Rest In Peace.

This is how I know that Keith is a murderer:

1. Divorce Settlements

When Keith "left" Margaret Clamwell there was no vicious court case and he came out of the marriage having lost nothing. Keith got all of the liquid and all of the illiquid assets. This means that he kept his house and his 1968 Triumph TR250 as well as the retirement plans and brokerage accounts (what are these?). This is not how divorce settlements work. In a marriage that does not end in murder, one partner will get the liquid assets and one partner will get the illiquid assets. Keith could only get both by murdering Margaret Clamwell. Which he definitely did.

2. Suspicious Mound

Keith used to live in a suburb called Sarahdale. The house he shared with Margaret Clamwell was number 7

Huntington Lane. If you go to this house late at night with a balaclava over your head and a torch in your hand, you will find a highly suspicious mound beneath an unenthusiastic apple tree. You will also be chased away and threatened by the current residents. This is where Keith buried Margaret Clamwell.

3. Body Type

Keith has the body type mesomorph; he is muscular and hard. William Sheldon did studies in the 1940s that showed how the temperament of mesomorphs may lead them to carry out crimes. Keith also has a handlebar mustache and could easily find employment in a gay bar. Gay people do murders a lot, like "The Doctor of Death." Keith is a Doctor of Death. Keith is a murderer.

4. Upbringing

Keith came from a "broken home." His dad beat him and his mother used heroin and his sister ran away to be a fake prostitute in a gothic circus. I know this because Keith enjoys telling me how easy my life is by talking about his childhood immediately after anything pleasant happens. I sometimes get the impression that he would like to break my home to teach me a lesson. Keith is also noticeably unintelligent. Both of these are risk factors in developing criminal tendencies. This means that you shouldn't blame Keith for what he did but you should be scared of him because he might murder you. This is why I need to get Keith away from Mum.

5. Confessions

Keith enjoys dropping subtle hints about how he murdered his wife through using clichéd phrases that relate to homicide. Some things he has said when discussing Margaret Clamwell are "It's all dead and buried now" and "I could have killed her." I know you killed her, Keith. Keith is a murderer.

+

I am trying to explain all of these evidences to Tenaya, again. It is Friday and we are sat in Lily's, on the comfy patched-up sofas by the bay window. It looks out onto a slim patchwork backstreet that holds a shop selling lavender soap and bath bombs, and a shop that sells Ouija boards, Buddhist books and incense. There is a pot of tea leaking steam between us and we are not holding cigarettes because the government have banned that. This year has been a bad year for good things.

"You can't be certain," she says. "Not yet. Wait a while, gather more evidence."

"This is enough evidence," I say. "He definitely did it."

Tenaya is a very practically minded person. She thinks things through very thoroughly. For this reason, Tenaya is either not entirely convinced of Keith's guilt or she is not entirely convinced that the police will be entirely convinced of Keith's guilt. Either one or both of these thoughts has prevented her from fully committing to my cause.

"We could exhume her?" Tenaya says.

I stare at her. My eyes are wide and excited. I can't understand why I didn't think of this. This is the perfect solution to the problem of incriminating Keith. We will dig up the body, call the police, and then Mum will be safe and Keith will be securely imprisoned.

"Fuck," I say. "Yes. I should have thought of that. When?"

"It will have to be a Saturday or a Sunday. It can't be tomorrow because of your party and it can't be next weekend because of the Psychology trip. That makes it either the twenty-fourth or the twenty-fifth, I think."

I am grinning at her now. I am excited about seeing justice done and also about getting to hold a dead body. A real dead human. A human that Keith killed, maybe with his bare hands or with a kitchen knife or a sawn-off shotgun or poison. There will maybe be a crater in Margaret Clamwell's skull where he hit her with a lamp or his trombone and she will maybe have fractured legs from where he broke them so she couldn't run away. The police will find out all of these things in the postmortem but I will find them out first.

We pay for our tea and walk to Imran's. Imran's is a corner shop run by several Indian men who all claim to be called Imran. We go there to buy alcohol and cigarettes because they always either fail to ask for ID or are susceptible to being convinced that we are overage. We are seventeen. Secret weapon: breasts.

Today it is the slovenly man with distinctly veined and protruding eyes. He is "reading" a men's magazine behind the counter, hurriedly tidying when we come in.

"Hello," Tenaya says. "Twenty-five grams of Gold Leaf and a liter of Chekhov, please."

The slovenly man examines us both. His eyes crawl even further out of his skull. I consider leaning forward, forcing them back in, and telling him that he is now free to lead a normal life.

"You got ID?" he asks. His voice is like the motor of an old Citroën.

"Sorry?"

"EYE DEE?"

"Oh, okay. Right. I'll have a look." Tenaya rummages in her pockets for the driving license that she does not have. "I don't have it. Fuck. I must have left it in the car. Are you going to make me go all the way back and get it?"

The man looks extremely uneasy.

He glances at me.

"EYE DEE?" he shouts.

"Sorry, I don't believe in carrying identification. Doing so means you are willingly embracing a totalitarian state."

The man blinks.

I have failed to abate his unease.

He turns back to Tenaya. Tenaya leans forward over the counter and presses her breasts together with her upper arms. She runs her tongue over her upper lip. I laugh. I bend the laugh into a cough. The cough climbs back out of my throat as more laughter.

The man sighs.

"You bring ID next time. You promise Imran this. Never again I do this, you hear?"

We nod. Greed defeats social responsibility. Everyone wins.

He puts the vodka into a blue plastic bag and passes Tenaya the tobacco.

We pay and leave.

So far the day's plans are unfolding well. As long as Ping gets the drugs for tomorrow and all the right people turn up then the party will go well. If something has gone well it means that I have had sex, gotten drunk and taken enough of a drug to feel the effects described to us by Mr. Gates during Personal Social Health Education. I feel quietly confident that all of these criteria will be fulfilled. The only criterion that is at all out of my control is the former, though this will be relatively easy to ensure, provided enough girls attend. If you fire enough shots then at least one will make contact, maybe more. Always exciting.

With the necessary personal supplies on board, we get the bus to Elsmere, where Mum and Keith are preparing for their visit to Keith's parents in Cornwall. They are having a pub party to celebrate their fiftieth wedding anniversary. They probably wouldn't want their son there if they knew the truth about him being a murderer. Then Mum wouldn't have to go either, which would be good for her because it will probably be shit. Keith will get drunk, say he loves her, convince her to do anal sex with him and then kill her. I hope he doesn't kill her. If he does, I will have concrete proof of his guilt. Ambivalence. Maybe he will try to worm his way out of the murder charge by claiming that her death was the result of an experimental sexual act gone wrong. People do that sometimes, I have seen it on the news.

"Hello, Jasper. Tenaya, dear, how are you?" Mum says. She is wrestling a suitcase into the boot of our mustard Volvo.

"Very well thank you, Mrs. Wolf," Tenaya says. When she speaks to my mum, Tenaya uses a voice she has stolen from a young girl in the television adaptation of a Dickens novel.

"Glad to hear it," Mum says. "Jasper, have you written out a schedule for your day tomorrow?"

Mum likes to write schedules. Tenaya says this is because she is a lawyer. I do not know if she is a lawyer or not. She has a briefcase and a BlackBerry. In Psychology we learned that retentive character traits are the result of underindulgence at the Anal Stage of Psychosexual Development. Mum constructs hugely detailed schedules and then suffers panic attacks when they are delayed because she needs the toilet or receives a phone call. By the time these panic attacks have subsided, her schedules have been so severely thwarted that she feels it necessary to write out new ones. Our house is littered with extremely dull schedules.

Here is a hypothetical example:

> 8:00–8:03 a.m. – Wake up, climb out of bed, tell Keith to get up.
> 8:03–8:10 a.m. – Brush teeth, go to the toilet, make a conscious effort to produce reeking feces.
> 8:10–8:45 a.m. – Eat breakfast. Encourage Jasper to write a schedule for the day. Incessantly quiz Jasper about schoolwork, girls, drugs and smoking. Attempt to dissuade Jasper from putting over one teaspoon of sugar into his tea. Inform Jasper that he is a colossal disappointment. Go to work.

This is a morning schedule. Mum will write three schedules every day: a work schedule, an evening schedule and a schedule for the following morning.

She constantly urges me to write schedules. During exam times and times when she is away I am *made* to write schedules. Both of these things are happening now. The writing of a schedule is unavoidable. I write two so as to keep us both content.

Here is the schedule that I show to Mum:

Revision Schedule (for Mum)
7:00 a.m. – Wake up, good morning! Breakfast of 2 Weetabix (sugarless)
7:30 a.m. – Revise, I will thank Mum one day!
11:00 a.m. – Therapy
12:30 p.m. – Further revision
6:00 p.m. – Dinner of lasagna and beans, get high on drugs (only joking, Mum!)
7:00 p.m. + Watch the History Channel / National Geographic / Discovery / other educational but exciting television channels in order to wind down before bedtime at 10:00 p.m.
Repeat.

Here is the schedule that I write for myself:

Revision Schedule (for me)
8:00 a.m. – Wake up if can be bothered. Breakfast of tea, four sugars, and cigarette
9:00 a.m. – Watch *Jeremy Kyle*
10:00 a.m. – Bath. Read *Mein Kampf* while bathing, try not to drop it!
11:00 a.m. – Therapy
12:15 p.m. – Collect Ping
12:30 p.m. – Talk over party details with Tenaya. Sit around.
4:00 p.m. – Move breakable objects. Deposit ashtrays on various surfaces. Leave plastic bowls beside beds and settees.

6:00 p.m. – Dine on curry-flavor Pot Noodles. Get high on drugs (sorry, Mum!)

8:00 p.m. – Graciously welcome guests and accept free cans of beer and cigarettes.

9:00 p.m. + Unstructured fun

Do not repeat.

"Are you staying over tonight, Tenaya?" Mum asks.

"If that's all right."

"Of course, just make sure your parents know where you are."

"Yes, Mrs. Wolf."

"And no one else is to come over."

"Yes, Mum."

Mum kisses me on the forehead and says that she loves me.

"Have a good time and make sure you two behave yourselves," she says, getting into our car.

"See you later, big man," Keith says.

"Yeah."

Keith often chooses to use oddly positive and patronizing colloquialisms when addressing me. On the occasions when he does address me, my internal monologue runs in overdrive, continually repeating the word *MURDERER* in the voice of a petrified middle-aged housewife. It is ironic that Keith uses so many friendly terms because actually he is brutal and heartless.

Mum told me once that I don't understand irony, which

was ironic because she was holding a packet of fish fingers at the time.

Not really, that was a joke. I was trying to lighten the mood.

Me and Tenaya watch the car shrink to nothing, then she rolls us both cigarettes and we go inside.

"Are the Layton Hill kids coming?" she asks. I shrug.

"Is Tom coming?" I ask. She shrugs.

"He said he would."

Tom is Tenaya's boyfriend. He wears knitted jumpers ironically and has oversized black plastic glasses. Sometimes, when Tom speaks, I can empathize with Keith and begin to believe that he may have had a valid reason for murdering Margaret Clamwell with his trombone. Tenaya only likes him because he has cheekbones like protractor edges.

"You had best be civil this time, Jasper," I am warned. Last time we were at a party with Tom, I put date-rape drug in his vodka and Tenaya had to carry him home. I later confessed under duress, because Tenaya was fretting that the vodka had been meant for her. She told me she was scared for her life.

"Of course," I promise. I have better plans for Tom this time.

We both begin to prepare the house for Saturday. We hide ornaments beneath the stairs and distribute ashtrays and buckets.

"Do you think people will feel compelled to break things?" I say.

"Depends."

"We should have some sort of system in place for dealing with offenders," I say. "If the house gets trashed, Mum will not let me get my nipple pierced."

"Your what?"

"Never mind."

"Did you say your nipple pierced, Jasper?"

"Do you still have that rape spray?"

"Your nipple?"

"Okay, we will rape-spray people in the eyes if they do anything wrong. You will trip them over and I will sit on their chests and spray them in their stupid vandal faces."

I throw some plastic bags around the room. They will save the family home my mother has worked so hard to provide for me.

"That should be fine," Tenaya says. "Do you have Julia tomorrow?"

"Yeah, you can stay here the whole day or meet me and Ping in town after, it's up to you."

"I'll decide in the morning."

Tenaya has enough ketamine left for us both to have a line. Mild relaxation ensues. We fall asleep watching a Royal Philharmonic rendition of Stravinsky's *Firebird.*

3

When I wake up the living room is choked with thick yellow light and it is cold. The television is still on, showing a tired woman selling Tupperware. I redistribute the duvet so that only Tenaya's head is left exposed. I make tea and start to run a bath.

According to my schedule, I should still be sleeping because it is 6:30 a.m. This means that if I bathe now I will have time to work on my novel before *Jeremy Kyle* starts. It is important that I continue to write things, even if they do not form anything coherent. If I write incoherent passages then I will be unlikely to write a seminal novel but it will be more likely than if I hadn't written at all.

The bath water is hot so all my blood rushes to the surface of the skin, as though it's trying to find out what is going on up there. Like when people all slow down to look at car accidents, my blood is fascinated by the misfortune of my skin. I put some of Mum's bath salts in so that the heat smells of lavender. The lavender heat makes me feel dizzy and calm. I am a relaxed and functioning human being. I read *Mein Kampf*.

For History, Mr. Glover always tells us to read certain chapters from the textbook. The textbook is a desert. It is "a pathway to exam success" but it is also not very useful if you want to understand history well. For example, when describing a racist man, the textbook may say "appeared to dislike those of color, often acted violently toward them" while the man's diary may read "their devilish hellskins blind me and eclipse the horizon." This is why I prefer reading the original literature of our notorious historical personalities.

Some choice quotes from *Mein Kampf* are:

— "All the human culture, all the results of art, science and technology that we see before us today, are almost exclusively the creative product of the Aryan."

I think that Hitler believed this because he never got a chance to listen to Wu-Tang Clan.

— "Halfway between man and ape."

I circled this. I thought it was funny. I showed it to Kobe during a free period and he laughed.

— "Men do not perish as a result of lost wars."

In Hitler's defense, I took this quote out of context. This quote is followed by something about men only perishing as a result of impure race. This was funny because of how America is the current favorite for "Winner of the Earth" and it is made up of immigrants from all over the world, breeding together in a phenomenally successful orgy of wealth and power.

I also read books written by people in the Ku Klux Klan when we were learning about them. I had to order the books from the Ku Klux Klan Web site and, because my order was over $25, they sent a free T-shirt that said WHITE KNIGHT WALKING and had a picture of a Klan member on a horse. Because it was an XL, I wore it to bed one night and Keith glimpsed it while I was brushing my teeth. The next day he had a secret conversation with Mum in the kitchen and she said, "Calm down, Keith, I'm sure it's just a phase, he'll grow out of it."

Choice quotes from Klan propaganda include:

— "Quarantine all AIDS carriers."
— "The false teachers of churchianity justify interracial marriages in order to keep the White race blind to administering God's laws."
— "We are the fog."

When the skin on my fingers folds up into origami swans, I get out of the bath and reclothe. Downstairs, I boil the kettle and sit down at the kitchen table with my notebook and a cigarette.

For a whole hour I work on a rape scene involving a man called Martin, who has a ginger beard and enjoys curry sauce, and a woman called Cindy, who only has seven toes and believes that the rape would stop if only she were able to expose them to Martin. Throughout the scene she attempts to remove her shoes while he penetrates her. She also tries to ward him off by repeatedly saying, "I only have seven toes." Martin doesn't care. Cindy begins to feel flattered by the rape. She feels as though someone really wants her and, for that, she gives herself up to Martin so that it stops being a rape and turns into just sex.

I feel ambivalent about the rape scene because it is poignant but also unbelievable. I tear out the pages and throw them into the bin. "Back to the drawing board," as Keith would say. The hour is not wasted however, as I have now decided that the novel should definitely contain a rape scene, maybe several.

Tenaya enters the kitchen. She sits down opposite me and starts to roll a cigarette. After she wakes up, her hair always makes it look as though she has just has passionate sex with a crack addict in a room with Velcro walls. Personally, I prefer it that way, but girls tend to have very distorted senses of self-image, so she doesn't listen to me when I tell her this.

"Your hair is nice like that," I say.

"Shut up, Jasper."

"I was being nice."

"How's the novel?" she asks.

Tenaya is very supportive of my ambitions. I have promised her that when I win the Booker Prize we will move to Eastern Europe and live off tea and toast.

"It's getting there," I assure her. "I am going to include a rape scene."

"Sarah DiLeeso was raped by a boy from Layton Hill who had a police tag round his ankle."

"Was she really?" I ask, fascinated. "Do you think she would consent to an interview?"

"*Jeremy Kyle* is starting," she says. She has ignored my question because it was inappropriate.

If someone tried to rape me then I would do my best to give them a hand job so that they cummed before they had torn my anus and would not want to go ahead with the rape. If this was not a viable option, however, then I might suggest that I was the "giver" and they were the "receiver" because that way it would be less painful for me. I might say things like, "You have been having a hard time lately, let me do the work," in order to persuade them.

We go back through to the living room and turn on *Jeremy Kyle*. It is a television program where the relationships of especially aggressive humans are repaired using intense circular arguments and lie detector tests. Tenaya asks to borrow a T-shirt, so I go and get my Ku Klux Klan one. She scowls as she pulls it on over her head. It reaches her knees. She is an eight-year-old dressed as Satan for Halloween.

The episode we are watching features a man called Jay and a woman called Kayler. They are both suffering severe acne. She is overweight and he is underweight. This is not the problem in their relationship. The problem in their relationship is that he smoked a lot of pot and then had sex with their dog, which she counts as cheating. He admits this but suggests that it is not cheating. They talk it over for a while. She makes him take a lie detector test because she believes he may be "a serial dog-raper."

Before the results of the test are revealed, I go upstairs to change for Julia. She often makes observations about my progress through how well-fitting and seemingly ironed my clothes are. I opt for blue skinny jeans and a white shirt. Mum would call this "presentable."

"Okay, I'm leaving now," I say.

"I'll stay here. In case you were wondering, Jay was lying about not being a serial dog-raper."

"Okay, thanks."

+

The sky is gray again. The sky is always gray in the suburbs. It is rarely, if ever, any real color between the hours of 10:00 a.m. and 9:00 p.m.

At the bus stop, I meet the old woman from number 26 who has schizophrenia. Mum scolded me once for laughing when I heard her talking about growing dogs from trees at the Village Fête.

They call it a Village Fête even though it is really a Suburb Fête.

This particular woman's name is Mrs Mulberry, and she believes that it is possible to grow humans from seeds made of paper tissue and urine. Me and Tenaya pressed our faces against her bay window once last year and the whole living room floor was covered in soil and tiny paper pellets.

We learned about schizophrenia in Psychology. It causes a distorted perception of reality. Mrs. Mulberry is remarkably original in her schizophrenia because she does not believe that a secret governmental organization / alien horde / religious cult is hunting her.

"Good morning, Mrs. Mulberry," I say.

"Hello, dear."

She has a vellum mustache and is wearing a blue mackintosh.

"How's the farming?"

"Not so well, I'm afraid. A nasty virus infected all the seeds and so I had to eat them so that I wouldn't grow children with Down's syndrome."

"I'm sorry. Maybe next season will yield a better crop. Did you know that people with Down's syndrome are technically a different species to us because they have a different number of chromosomes?"

"Flat-faced rats," she says.

I feel uncomfortable with Mrs. Mulberry's commentary but, in line with Mother's wishes, I nod and smile.

The bus pulls up. It is being driven by the bus driver with dreadlocks like old kebabs. I go up and sit on the top deck so that Mrs. Mulberry can't follow me. For a while after the bus starts, I hear a distressed scratching sound that means Mrs. Mulberry is trying to follow me up the stairs using her walking stick and broken Meccano knees. Eventually she sighs and sits down on the bottom floor.

I have had a therapist since me and Tenaya were caught killing a cat. We only killed the cat because I accidentally fell on it and it was in a lot of pain. I killed it with my foot. Tenaya was not appointed a therapist because her mother could not afford one and also because she insisted that animal abuse was perfectly normal for children of our age. She said that we must have been testing the boundaries of our relationship with the natural world. My mother said that Tenaya's mother was a "fat hippie whore" and Tenaya's mother said that my mother was a "rich bitch."

My therapist is an art therapist called Julia. She insists I call her Julia and not "Mrs. Hawthorn," so that I view her as a friend and open up to her, which I do not.

Julia is pleasant and naive. She believes everything that I tell her.

I am watching the sky melt into puddles on the tarmac through Julia's small window. She has already asked about

Sebastian (I have confided in Julia that I am a homosexual in a long-term relationship), *Cunnilingual* (I have confided in Julia that I write short stories for an erotic magazine) and meditation (I have confided in Julia that I practice Mahayana Buddhism and am nearing partial enlightenment).

"Have you had any more dark thoughts recently, Jasper?" she says.

Sugar is pouring out of her lips. Sugar is only good when it is in tea. It is not good when it is coming out of the mouths of overpaid women in suits who think that they are emotionally shampooing me.

Julia leans in.

Her thin face is folded in a way that suggests she used to be attractive and hasn't yet realized that she no longer is. She has green eyes and cropped blonde hair, the kind of cut that middle-aged women ask for when they want to look like Victoria Beckham. Julia does not look like Victoria Beckham. Julia looks like Susan Boyle.

"I saw a snail this morning and wanted to crush it under my foot but then I thought about how doing so would prevent the snail from having future pleasurable life experiences, so I stepped over it instead."

She weakly pats her hands against each other in understated feminine applause.

"See, Jasper? I told you we could make progress. You just need to remember to imagine yourself in the shoes of others."

I nod.

"Empathy," she says.

"Empathy," I repeat.

Julia removes a sheet of paper from beside my folder. My folder is where she writes down all of the lies I have told her in the past year.

The sheet of paper has three ovals on. Each oval has been given a name: Sebastian, Mum, Keith. Julia asks me to draw onto each oval the expression that best illustrates my feelings toward the person.

When I first visited the therapy clinic, I was promised that art therapy is a "healing" and "life-enhancing" practice, whose effectiveness has been scientifically proven with research studies of large samples. I am an experienced user of Google and still could not find any of these studies. In reality, art therapy is patronizing, or it would be were I to embrace it seriously. Julia thinks she is patronizing me, and I think I am humoring Julia, so sessions swing like carousels and fairgrounds, and are very exciting.

I draw a winking face with a quiff on Sebastian's oval, a smiling face with curly hair on Mum's, and a mustached face doing a thumbs-up on Keith's. Julia nods encouragingly. The right answer.

After an entire hour of drawing faces, animals, buildings and "abstract objects which represent tangible feelings," I am told to stop.

Julia is smiling.

"I think we have definitely made progress. Do you think we have made progress, Jasper?" she asks.

"Yes, Julia. I think I have progressed well. I feel like a healthy, well-balanced individual, thanks to your care and attention."

She blushes. Her cheeks are empty poppy fields.

"How is the Klan?" she asks.

A month ago, I decided to put my Ku Klux Klan T-shirt to good use by wearing it to a therapy session and telling Julia I had joined. I explained to her that I held bimonthly meetings in my bedroom with other Klansmen from around Ivythorne.

"Are there many Klansmen in Ivythorne?" she had asked.

"Yes, lots. Do you remember that prominent local Afro-Caribbean artist who died last year?"

"Yes, John Ducell. He died of cancer."

"Oh, okay."

Julia opened her mouth and stretched her eyes very wide when I said this. Then she changed the subject.

"It is going well, thank you," I tell her. "Next week we are going to spray graffiti on the Caribbean social club."

Every time Julia fails to spot my lies or to dissuade me from engaging in hate crimes, I feel a sinking disappointment in the year 2010. I do not like the way people act now. Mr. Hutchinson calls it "the plague of the postmodern era." The plague is tolerance. The plague is being made to tolerate even the intolerant. This is why you can go to www.KKK.com and buy T-shirts with White Power slogans on them.

The Internet is good because you can watch niche porn for free but bad because you can buy racist clothing.

Julia moves two sheets of paper from one side of her desk to the other.

"Ooh, look, time's up," she says, grinning. "Have a good weekend, Jasper."

"Thanks."

Outside the Oaktree Center I roll a cigarette and call Ping. He tells me to meet him in McDonald's. An Asian boy walks past and goes through the automatic glass doors with black tree motifs on them. He is wearing short shorts and silver trainers and he is scratching his hands. Long scabs like kite tails trail up his arms. It looks painful.

When I reach McDonald's, I find Ping reclining amongst a dystopian wasteland of burger wrappers and flaccid ketchup sachets. He is texting. I wonder who he is texting. He doesn't see me enter, so I stand behind him and alert him to my presence by hitting his head hard and saying, "Coco bongo!"

"Fuck off, gayboy," he says, turning to face me.

I grin.

"Let's go," I say.

4

"Hey, man," Jonah says. He has just arrived in Elsmere.

We are at the 38 bus stop, collecting partygoers. There appear to be around twenty-one boys and three girls.

"This is going to be a fucking sausagefest," Ping says.

"It will be fine," I tell him. "More girls will come later. Lots and lots of girls. So many girls that it will inevitably turn into an orgy."

Jonah laughs.

"Yeah, man, bare gash."

Jonah wears tight girls' jeans and his earlobes are stretched with big Perspex plugs. He says that they are fourteen millimeters wide. Tenaya says that they are disgusting and because of them he will cease to get sex after thirty. He says that she is jealous.

"There's a party in the valley," Ben McKay says. "A load of people went to that."

"Fucking brilliant," Ping says.

Jonah gives us both cans of beer and says that everything will definitely be okay.

It is approximately eight o'clock. I do not know the exact time because I have left my phone at home. I feel anxious when I do not know the exact time. The sky is wholly dark and the tungsten streetlights are dropping maps of orange light onto the pavements. Our beers are extremely cold, which is unfortunate because the night is also not warm.

We see two boys in tracksuits beneath one of the streetlights near the end of Ivythorne Road. They look disproportionately intimidating for their ages, around fourteen.

"Fuck," Ping says.

Jonah tells him not to be a pussy.

We start to walk past the boys.

"Nice ears, mate," one of them shouts to Jonah. "I could fit my fucking dick through those things."

They both laugh.

"Good for you, babydick," Jonah shouts back.

They stop laughing.

The one with the white tracksuit on cycles over.

"What the fuck did you say?"

"Babydick," Jonah repeats, smiling.

Ping groans.

The one with the white tracksuit on wraps his arm around Jonah's neck, bringing him down into a headlock while the one with the navy tracksuit on cycles over. I begin to wonder what is going through their heads. There are more than twenty of us and two of them. They are mindless predators.

"Fucking burn him," the one with the white tracksuit says. The one with the navy tracksuit flicks up the flame of a lighter and begins to move it toward Jonah's peroxide hair. What are they doing?

"What? NO, do something!" Jonah is screaming and struggling. "Ping? Ben? Fucking help!"

There are twenty of us but we are just stood there. Then someone shouts "RUN!" and everyone is gone, except for me and Tenaya. She is holding a lit cigarette and smiling, as though she has a foolproof plan. We both watch while Jonah begins to lose his fringe. It must be a bad time to be Jonah. I feel bad for him but I am also glad it is him and not me.

"Why the fuck aren't you doing something?" he shouts.

Tenaya steps toward the one in the white tracksuit and puts her cigarette out on the inside of his ear.

I see it glow red.

The boy is screaming.

Jonah is free.

We run back to the house and fall through the door and collapse on the sofa. My chest is a coalless steam train. I am dizzy. Jonah touches his hair, shudders, and starts rolling a joint.

"Shit," he says.

"Yeah," Tenaya agrees.

"Thanks."

We pass around the joint. We make use of the three-toke pass system in order to share it fairly. Relaxation ensues.

"It's not that bad, right?" Jonah asks, fringe between his fingers.

"Barely noticeable," Tenaya says.

I think it is noticeable but I do not say anything. I am sometimes extremely sensitive.

"Thank fuck."

There is a knock at the door. When I answer, I find the deserters, all drunk and smiling. Three small cars pull up and I feel momentarily worried but they turn out only to contain Sarah DiLeeso and a bunch of other kids from the year above. I am sure that everyone will treat my family home with the respect that it deserves. These are not the kind of people that steal your cutlery and urinate in your bath.

We all go inside.

An hour later and four girls are mixing vodka on the carpet. Someone is playing hip-hop through the surround sound. There are two boys kissing on the sofa. The music is Wu-Tang Clan. The song is "Shame On A Nigga." I can hear Sarah DiLeeso and Jonah singing.

Me and Ping go through to the kitchen to cook up ketamine. He is drunk and so attempting to engage me in philosophical conversation, which is something he is not very good at.

". . . so we must have a soul because due to the, uh, sheer number of human traits that can't be accounted for, you know, genetically or . . ."

Ping does this a lot. He is sort of an idiot.

I nod while he slips the clear liquid from its cellophane glove into a pan. I open a beer. We both take up seats on the marble worktops and I light a cigarette.

"Apparently Abby Hall has a thing for you," Ping says.

A hairpin change of topic.

Abby Hall is a plump blonde girl with bright trails of acne up her cheeks who insists on wearing leggings despite the width of her calves. She believes in angels and does not drink. At parties she binges on Red Bull and talks without breathing.

"You are joking."

"I am not joking."

I mentally conjure a naked lineup of the girls that are present. Abby Hall is smiling and juggling her acned breasts. The Jewish girls are all telling me to look away. Emma Howes is massive. Ana Korsakov looks nice. She would definitely get it. I omit the girls with boyfriends.

"And don't try Ana," Ping says. "It's already a done deal."

He winks. He winks to make it clear to me that he is talking about sexual things.

Ana Korsakov is poor. She gets Christmas presents from the Salvation Army.

I promise myself that I will masturbate if no other girls turn up. This will ensure that I do not plump (sorry) for a fat girl whom I will later regret.

"I'd just go with Abby," Ping says.

"Right," I say. "Except you wouldn't."

He laughs.

"I would if I looked like you."

"Yeah," I say. "Great. Anyway, I will be seducing Georgia Treely in Devon. She is way fitter than Ana."

Ping laughs. "Okay."

I can hear Die Antwoord playing in the living room now. Die Antwoord are a rap band from South Africa. They say things like "next-level shit." In Careers I wanted to write that down on my "hopes for the future" form. Tenaya told me that if I did, the Careers Officer would think that I had taken LSD and she would phone Mum. I nodded and wrote "children's television presenter" instead.

I go back into the living room. One of the gay boys on the sofa is giving the other a hand job. Ana Korsakov and her chubby friend are watching and laughing. The room is littered with embracing couples who think that they are happy. My bladder is a hot-air balloon. I go upstairs to use the toilet and pass Tenaya and Tom arguing, which makes me secretly optimistic but I am too sensitive to say anything. What a sensitive mood I am in today. I decide not to give him the Viagra.

Ben McKay is sleeping in the bath, in a halo of fluorescent vomit. I treat myself to a sitting-down piss, take his cigarettes and go back downstairs. I do not like Ben McKay. Ben McKay likes Coldplay.

"It's done, man," Ping says.

We tip the drugs out of the pan and into a small white heap on the turquoise marble. He takes out his debit card and we chop up two lines then hoover them through rolled-up five-pound notes. I do not feel any effects after the first line. Ping is laughing. After eight lines I feel something.

+

I am a wolf. Jasper James Wolf. Look at me. How beautiful I am. So sleek and slender. I have great hair. I am pretty powerful. Also, I am sinking. Perhaps I am walking over the ocean. The kitchen tiles are ice. I can overcome them with my wit. Wit surpassing Stephen Fry. Come on, girls, look at my beautiful eyes. You can stroke me if you like. This music is lemonade in my veins. Maybe I should dye my hair ginger. My fur. I don't know my own strength. I should refrain from touching people where possible. That's it, climbing the stairs. This is enjoyable. I am enjoying myself. I also feel nauseous and sleepy. Quite sleepy. Sleepy eight on a one-to-ten scale of sleepiness. That is beatable. Especially with such power as I have been endowed. Thank you, sun. Oh, toilet. Hello, Abby Hall. Shush, we shouldn't speak. Yes, I am beautiful. You can tell me with your hands. Let's lie in here. In the bath. Oh, Ben McKay is here. Vomit on your leggings? Take them off. Everything is going to be okay. I promise. I will make many promises to you. I know my claws are vicious. Your mouth is mine. Giggling. Inside of your eyes. My claws are making you sing. You sing like a haunting. Isn't everything glowing? This is very nice. Hello, Abby Hall. Yes, around your feet. Just throw them to Ben McKay. To the lions! I am a wolf, you know. This must make you very happy. Yes, it does. You're moaning agreement. Princess. You are my princess. I am your wolf. We are on the bathroom floor. We should dispense with the clawing, though you pull well. Let us run through flesh fields. What? Oh, no matter. I am a wolf, I can cope with wearing a little blood. I have blood, you have blood. Your blood on me. Me inside of . . . oh, this is . . . Let's move. Let's move to bed. My parents' bed. Super Super King Queen Size. Yes, this is velvet beneath us. Union. Duet. The flute and the French horn. Oh. Yes. This. Thank you. Your thighs are waterslides. A furry theme park. Smack the weasel. Oh. Yes. Your blood on the sheets. Turn over. I am in the arch of your neck. This is sunshine. We are alive. Hello, Abby Hall.

+

It is 5:16 a.m. My throat is a desert filled with pesticides. My head is a motorway. I am lying next to Abby Hall. I appear to have stolen all the duvet sometime during the last few hours. Her breasts are drooping down her chest like bags of goldfish from a fair. Her nose is blocked so that when she breathes it sounds like a cat purring.

Last night is going to follow me for weeks. Like a pedophile, or Keith, stalking their victims.

I stand up. There is blood on and in the immediate vicinity of my penis. This is the most disgusting I have felt ever in my life. Ever. The immediate future will only prove at all bearable provided Abby Hall remains sleeping. Plump Abby Hall with her obnoxious breasts and acne.

Oh, Jesus.

You did it wrong, Jasper. Georgia Treely is the only female in the world.

Downstairs, I find Tenaya. Her eyes are all swollen up and bloodshot. She is sitting between two stacks of discarded tissues and there is an old copy of collected Sartre essays on the table.

"Good morning," I say. My voice is weighed down by the bloody ghost of my past.

"Morning," she replies.

She throws me a pair of jeans from the floor. I pull a

full condom off them and climb in. They look like maybe they could be a girl's. Nothing matters. No future.

"I'll make coffee and cigarettes, then we can sit outside and you can explain," I tell her.

She nods. It is a very faint nod.

I roll our cigarettes while the kettle boils. Someone has built a railway in my head. I built the railway in my head. I built it with cheap wine and horrible sex. Horrible, horrible sex. I can see the ghost of last night's drug of choice on the marble worktop. There are several people sleeping on the kitchen tiles, which I imagine must be particularly uncomfortable but they appear not to mind. Ana Korsakov and Ping are curled up on Keith's yellow towel underneath the kitchen table. There is a pool of blood and a steak knife in the sink. Weird.

Ping's eyes half open as the kettle climaxes.

I don't mind that Ping reserved Ana Korsakov for himself because she doesn't like me anyway. This is because when she had a party last summer, I punched her pit bull and gave it a black eye. It was exciting. She called me a "*sukr*." She told me this was Russian for bitch.

"Morning," he says, standing up.

"Yeah."

"I feel ill."

"You and Ana?"

Ping massages his eyelids. We both look down at the small, unkempt girl asleep across his legs.

"Don't know," he whispers. "I mean, I really like her,

man, just, I can't put my dick in, you know, her being nice and shit."

"You didn't do sex?"

"Russian Orthodox."

"She'll have to give in eventually."

"I fucking hope so. We're playing at the Twelve Cats next week, maybe after that."

Ping is in a ska band who sing songs about marijuana.

"Maybe."

I make three teas, leave one on the side for Ping, and go back through to the living room.

"Here," I say, passing Tenaya her coffee and cigarette. "It's the good tobacco."

We go outside to sit on the decking but move to the trampoline after Tenaya declares that she is uncomfortable. We lie on our backs and light the cigarettes.

Morning is making early promises from the edge of the world and the sky directly over our heads is the color of blue Slush Puppie. It is cold but the cold feels invigorating and not murderous. My head is labeling these things and not properly acknowledging them.

"This tea is gash, Jasper," she says.

"Sorry," I say. "Tell me what happened. It was to do with Tom."

"I know you didn't like him, Jasper," Tenaya begins. "But I thought he was wonderful."

"I know you thought he was wonderful, Tenaya," I say. "But he was a massive dick."

She pulls up her upper body and punches my collar-bone.

"He broke up with me."

"What should I do with all that Viagra?"

She punches me again.

"Why?" I ask.

She lies back down.

"You heard us arguing last night?"

"Yeah."

"Well, that was because Rajid told me that Tom had gone down on Alice Jennings and I was confronting him about it. I felt unsure as to how true it was because Rajid didn't seem too sure." Alice Jennings is one of the rich Jewish girls. She wears Ugg boots and back-combs her hair. "We were arguing about it and then Jonah walks past and says, 'Oh, she found out then?'"

Tenaya takes a very pronounced drag on her cigarette.

"But you said that he broke up with you?" I say.

"Well . . . I was going to forgive him."

I am unsure of what scoffing really sounds like but I make a good attempt at what I think it must entail by blowing hard out of my nose. Some snot comes out and lands on my bare chest. I wipe it off with the underside of my coffee mug.

"Well, I didn't think it meant anything and I really do like him. Anyway, after a while he said, 'I know you are probably considering forgiving me but I could never forgive myself, so I think this is over.'"

This causes me to laugh quite uncontrollably.

Tenaya begins to cry.

Her tears wage a war on my laughter.

She wins.

They call the victory guilt.

I hold Tenaya's hand and we both stop making emotional sounds. God has been diluting the Slush Puppie sky so that bright light is showering us.

"Why is there blood and a steak knife in the sink?" I say.

Tenaya smiles.

"Some girls from the valley party came up because theirs was closed down, and one of them tried to stab Jonah because she said he was trying to rape her, except she slipped on some Irn-Bru he had spilled on the floor and cut off her own finger."

"Oh," I say. "Right." This is both hilarious and unnerving. "I had been keeping the Viagra dissolved in a bottle of Irn-Bru."

Tenaya snorts with laughter.

"You actually had Viagra? I told you to be civil."

"Doesn't matter now. Anyway, then what happened?"

She takes a while to regain her composure.

"Then Emma Howes put the finger in a fridge pack of Fosters and drove the girl to the hospital but she didn't make it because she was drunk and she skidded the car into a ditch. She phoned Jonah and he left, like, a half hour ago to tow them out."

We both sit up, facing the bottom of the garden. The rabbits are waking up and patrolling their hutch perimeters. Our rabbits are named after the Teenage Mutant Ninja Turtles: Raphael, Donatello, Michelangelo and Leonardo. I wanted to name them after the Biker Mice from Mars but there are only three of them.

"Where did you go?" she asks.

"Nowhere. Me and Ping had that ketamine, then I felt tired and went to bed."

Tenaya does a thing sometimes where she raises her eyebrows and flares her nostrils because she does not believe what I have told her. This is what she is doing now.

"Okay, fine. That isn't what happened. I was mashed on K and I had sex with Abby Hall, even though she is plump and even though she was on her period."

I put my head in my hands while Tenaya erupts. Her eruption was predictable; that is why I have hidden my ears with my hands.

Two thick, hairy arms wrap around me from behind and a pair of warm lips kiss my neck. I hear Abby Hall say, "Morning, baby." Tenaya re-erupts. Jonah emerges from the house and also erupts. I try to convince my heart to stop.

5

When we have gotten everyone to leave, Tenaya tells me to go and sleep. I am too tired to argue. I turn Radio 4 on low and fall asleep to the sound of a man explaining about the speed of the Internet in rural Iraq.

Tenaya tidies while I am asleep so that when Mum and Keith get back they are pleasantly surprised.

Keith is sipping coffee in his dressing gown when I go downstairs in the evening. He is reading *The Da Vinci Code*. Keith is illiterate.

"Hi," I say.

(Murderer)

"Hello," Keith says.

(Murderer)

"Did you have a good time in Cornwall?"

(Did you kill anyone in Cornwall?)

"Yes, thanks, it was nice actually."

("I killed and raped several innocent pensioners.")

"Good."

(I am going to call the police on you and you will be locked away for life, which is fifteen years and actually only seven if you refrain from raping anyone in jail.)

"And the party was dead good."

(Too easy)

"Yeah?"

(Murderer)

"Yeah, I think your mum had a good time."

("I slayed her with my skinsword, and then with a real sword, and then ate her in a lasagna.")

"Where is she?"

(What have you done with her?)

"She's upstairs in the bath."

(A bath of her own blood)

"Okay," I say. "I'll see you tomorrow."

My head is still somersaulting so I go back into my room and lie down. I turn on the laptop and use it to repeatedly check various social networking sites for signs that people have remembered I am still alive. Nobody has.

I think about working on my novel but instead I play naked computer solitaire for an hour then fall asleep.

+

I wake early, dress for school, and go downstairs for breakfast. Mum has made me a sugarless tea. She thanks me for having looked after the house and then leaves for work. Keith has already left. Before I embark on the six-minute walk to school, I go to the shed in order to retrieve my cigarettes, lighter and hopefully some marijuana debris. I find one of the Layton Hill kids laid in the corner beneath my old coat, having apparently only just regained consciousness and repeatedly mumbling that he is "Hungry, so fucking hungry." Interestingly, the boy has had the crotch of both his jeans and boxer shorts cut out. I lead him up the garden, force a piece of bread into his hands and guide him out the front door, ahead of me and in the opposite direction.

St. Mary's is a well-respected grammar school with several awards and enviable statuses to its name. Layton Hill is a comprehensive school with a remarkably lax penal system and a bustling trade in illegal drugs. Mum said that she would sooner home-tutor me than send me there. I wouldn't mind. Both schools look like plastic prisons and smell of Plasticine.

First period we have Religious Studies with Mrs. Norton. She is a wrinkled woman who wears hemp clothes with wooden beads and is very scared for the future of our damned souls. She tells us this on a regular basis. Roughly once a week. Ping has dubbed her "Most Likely to Fuck a Student and Later Confess, Seeking a Lenient Sentence on the Grounds That It Was 'God-Ordained Love.'"

Mrs. Norton appears to have dispensed with greetings and is stood at the front of the class clutching one of the old projectors. She is gripping so hard that the skin on her hands has lost its blood and is beginning to look like a dead man's testicles. Jonah has his hand raised and is being ignored.

"HEATHENS," she shouts, "we are such lost lambs. We are so cold and alone here." Mrs. Norton is mentally ill. This is a badly kept secret.

Ping and Jonah are already laughing.

"Our skies are coal. Our feet are thorns. Seek ye the Lord while he may be found!"

Tenaya takes out the Ha Jin novel she is midway through.

I feel vaguely interested in where Mrs. Norton is going with this today. She has been known to wind her lectures up in a great number of different ways.

"Look at me, all of you. Look and believe. Call down the power of God and channel it into this projector."

Oh.

"You must all believe, you must hold fast your faith with all your might."

Ping has turned around and is speaking to Sarah Fields.

Jonah is using his phone.

"You need to believe, call God down now, to stand among us men."

Mrs. Norton's first name is Acacia, which is a type of spiny bush.

"Mark 9, 23: Everything is possible for him who believes."

Seems unbelievable, right?

"You must hold this projector in the air with your faith."

I wince.

It actually happened.

When the projector falls, the arm shatters and the body crushes Mrs. Norton's foot. She begins to scream and shout, "A class of the damned!"

Me and Tenaya get up and leave.

We go out the front of the school to have cigarettes at the 61 bus stop.

Once, Mrs. Norton threw all of our pencil cases out of the window, one by one, claiming that we might use the power of God to save them from a splintered fate. Ana's nan lodged a formal complaint against her and the school sent Mr. Golding to observe our lessons. This meant that, for a week, we had a series of real lessons that involved interpreting biblical passages and applying them to serious ethical issues of the day. When Mr. Golding had left appeased, Mrs. Norton had thrown Ana's whole bag out of the window and Ana had changed Religious Studies for Sociology.

"Why hasn't she been fired?" I ask Tenaya.

"Because she can teach."

"But she doesn't."

"But she can. Besides, everyone gets through the exam by learning the textbook."

Ping wanders out of school holding his crushed pack of Marlboro Lights.

"How did you enjoy that, loverboy?" he says.

"What happened?"

"She broke her foot. Maybe both feet. Jonah is driving her to the hospital."

"What? Why is Jonah taking her?"

"All of the teachers said they were busy. Anyway, seen Abby?"

"No. Why?"

"You seem to have set her on fire, you fucking chubby-chaser. She is telling everyone about what happened." He grins. "The Bloody Baron," he says. He wiggles his fingers like people do when they do ghost impressions even though ghosts don't have fingers really.

I groan.

If Abby doesn't leave me alone then I will have to form a plan to defend myself. Were she to come on the Psychology trip and the end-of-exams Devon trip, wrapping her moss-log arms around me and kissing my neck, then it will likely ruin them. She would ruin The Georgia Plan. Watching me be fondled by Abby Hall is not seductive.

At times the best form of defense is offense. I will have to bear that in mind.

"It was a bit weird," Tenaya says.

I don't answer.

Abby Hall comes out of the school gates. She runs up

to me with her giantess legs quivering, steals my cigarette and throws it to the ground.

"That's a filthy habit, Jasper. If you want to keep me, you will have to give it up."

Due to excessive cowardice, inherited from my father, I am extremely scared of directly inflicting emotional injury. For this reason, during the six minutes in which Abby Hall embraces me and puts her kisses on my cheeks, I say nothing. She squeezes my buttock with her hand and bites her lip. Tenaya and Ping are grinning at each other. The bell rings for second period and we all go back into school.

In Period 2, we have Psychology. This means that I learn nothing because I am sat behind Georgia Treely. I watch her hair reflect the cheap striplights. She raises her hand more often than other people. There are plastic beads around her wrists. The wrists are erogenous zones. Her wrists are especially erogenous zones. Georgia Treely is a devout Catholic, a stubborn vegetarian and a generous philanthropist. Tenaya says that for these reasons it is surprising that I find her attractive; however, these are not the things that I find attractive about her. The things I find attractive about her are: the arches of her cheekbones, her eyelashes, the slim "hourglass" shape of her body, her ankles, her small feet, her breasts, her hair, her neck and her mouth. She is a collage of the best body parts in *Vogue*.

I am not shallow; healthy body, healthy mind.

When Psychology ends, I have learned two things: Georgia Treely has a new Winnie the Pooh fountain pen, and Georgia Treely has a new yellow plastic bracelet.

I leave after Psychology because it is only PE after lunch. Nobody is at home. I go up to my room to plot.

6

8:02 p.m. I am at Tenaya's. Tenaya is in the shower. Tenaya's mum is asleep next to me on the sofa with the soles of her bare feet pressed against my right thigh. Her legs are freckled with the beginnings of black hairs. She looks like a large, tired child.

The first Harry Potter film is playing on the television. A flock of bright boats are shifting over black water. I have seen this film more times than I have had sex. That is a statistic I need to reverse. I will begin by not watching it again.

I make sure not to nudge Tenaya's mum as I stand up. She probably wouldn't notice anyway. She probably wouldn't wake up even if I pulled her hair and licked her ears. Alcohol is unhealthy because when you get drunk and fall asleep, you don't remember what you did in your dreams.

Sometimes I feel very guilty about the things I have done in my dreams. I have hurt people the most during sleep, and it doesn't matter if they know or not.

Tenaya is sat on the bed in her room on the third story when I go up. She has a towel pulled around her, pushing her breasts against her chest. They spill out over the top like the foreheads of curious children. Her wet hair hugs the shape of her head. She shouts my name and tells me to get out.

Too slow.

On the other side of the door I sink onto the carpet. I look at the lines on my hands. Something just happened very quickly. I do not know what to do. She was too slow and I saw. There are columns of long nicks across her upper arms. What does that mean? I have heard about people who cut themselves, on the radio. It did not make sense to me.

I knock on her bedroom door. She doesn't say anything. I knock again.

"Tenaya," I say.

"Yes."

"Can I come in now?"

"Fine."

She's changed into a dress and a cardigan when I go in. I sit on the edge of her bed. Self-harm is a phase that many adolescents pass through, the radio said. It is often a cry for help.

"Do you want help?" I say.

"With what?"

The radio didn't say. "With your arms."

"Do I want help with my arms?"

"Well, I don't know."

"Can we just not?"

"Okay."

I get up and turn the television on. It is on the same channel as the one downstairs. Harry Potter. Tenaya attacks herself. The Great Hall is filled with beaming children taking bites out of large steaks. We arrange ourselves. I prop myself up against pillows and Tenaya lies flat on her front, calves in the air. It is sometimes best to hide in places you have never been.

+

When I wake up it is 11:14 p.m. I shake Tenaya until her eyes open. She hits herself in her eye, trying to get moondust out. Then she pulls her skirt down and sits up.

"I'm hungry," I say.

"Yeah."

"I'm making tea."

"I'll be down in a minute."

I walk the four flights of stairs down to the kitchen in the basement. It is a calm, dark bunker. A single naked lightbulb throws a dim yellow against the walls. It is an energy-saving lightbulb. Tenaya's parents think it is a planet-saving lightbulb. I think it is too late to save the planet.

The kettle boils loudly because it is angry at being woken up. I give Tenaya the Harry Potter cup and take a wonky brown one her mum made at a pottery workshop for me, then I roll two cigarettes and arrange everything on the table. I am being considerate. I will make Tenaya feel safe and comfortable so that I can find out why she is making cries for help.

She comes down the stairs, does a small smile, and takes a seat opposite me. She takes a sip of her tea to see how hot it is. I put my finger in mine.

"Can we talk about your arms now?" I say.

Tenaya lights one of the cigarettes. She rests her head in her hand. "No."

"Why are there cuts on your arms?"

"Jasper."

"I heard about self-harming on the radio. They said it was a common way of asking for help." I try my best to make a smile. "Can I help?"

"I didn't do it for a reason."

"Then why?"

"I don't know."

I light my cigarette and sip the tea. Tenaya's hands look smaller than I have ever seen them and they are shaking. The bones in them stand out like cocktail sticks under her skin.

"Is it Tom still?"

"Not everything has a reason, Jasper."

"Is Tom the reason?"

"Maybe."

I look hard into her eyes, like policemen do on the television when they know a witness is hiding something.

"Are you okay?"

She doesn't say anything. She looks down into her mug. I try to imagine what a man in a film would do. A man in a film would lean forward and tilt her head upward and see something in her eyes that explains everything. I think if I do that, Tenaya will hit me.

She crushes out her cigarette and looks up.

"It happens sometimes," she says. "I don't know why. Sometimes I just feel not well. I don't know. It isn't because of Tom. It isn't because of anything. That's the point, I think. Maybe it is Tom. I don't know, Jasper. Sorry."

"Oh." I don't know what to say. I am being confronted with real human emotions. I should do something. I want to do something. "Does anything help?" I say.

"People," she says. "When there are people here."

"Okay. Then text me when you feel like that, please."

"Thanks, Jasper."

"We just had a serious talk."

Tenaya laughs. She downs the last of her tea and stands up.

"Are you hungry still?"

"A bit."

"Beans on toast?"

"Thanks."

I roll more cigarettes while she makes toast and microwaves beans. Her shadow flashes across the kitchen tiles. She will be a good wife. A good wife and a good mother and a good adult. She will get better. I will try to surround her at all times until she does.

We eat quietly with Radio 4 on. Once I have finished, I decide to find out if I will become a father.

"Tenaya," I say, "out of interest, can girls get pregnant on their periods?"

She tries not to laugh. "No," she says. "Well, it is basically impossible."

I AM NOT GOING TO BE A FATHER. I HAVE WON THE LOTTERY.

"Why?" she says.

"Isn't it obvious?"

"Abby?"

"Yes."

Tenaya bites her lip. "You weren't told?"

"Told what?"

"Abby wasn't on her period. It was her first time."

"What?"

"Her hymen, Jasper. You smashed her flower."

Oh, fucking hell. I am still going to maybe be a father.

No.

No, I absolutely am not.

It would not be allowed to happen.

However, I do now have an idea for removing Abby Hall from Devon and ensuring the success of The Georgia Plan.

"Is there any wine?"

Fucking flower-smasher.

"In the fridge."

"Can we go upstairs now?"

"Okay."

Back upstairs Tenaya falls asleep midway through an episode of *Gilmore Girls*. I try to decide: Loralai or Rory. I can't. I turn on Tenaya's laptop and play Minesweeper and I get a new best time for intermediate but that doesn't mean anything because Tenaya is shit at Minesweeper.

7

It is Tuesday afternoon. We have finished school and me and Tenaya are sat in Lily's with a pot of tea between us. She is wearing long sleeves. She tried to go straight home after school and I told her she couldn't.

I show her my plan for keeping Abby Hall away from the upcoming events. It is in letter form.

Dear Abby Hall,

We are writing to inform you that despite heavy illegal drug use during early pregnancy, your prenatal test has shown up no signs of defective genes or chromosomal abnormalities in your fetus.

It may also interest you to know that the relative

elasticity of your labia, as caused by frequent intercourse, will mean that labor itself will prove relatively painless.

We wish you the best of luck with your gestation and look forward to seeing you in March!

Ramad Chankrih
Head of Babies and Drugs and Stuff at the hospital on London Road

Tenaya laughs and some tea dribbles out of her nostril.

"Nobody would believe a doctor said that," she says. "Defective genes and chromosomal abnormalities are not caused by heavy drug use."

"Her parents don't know that."

"Of course they do. I know that."

"So?"

"Doctors don't use exclamation marks."

"Enthusiastic doctors do."

"You wrote the phrase 'elasticity of your labia,' Jasper." She raises her eyebrows. "Nobody would believe a doctor said that."

"Yes, they would, it's scientific phrasing."

Tenaya picks up the letter and proceeds to read from it, laughing.

"'Ramad Chankrih, Head of Babies and Drugs and Stuff at the hospital on London Road.' And that?"

"It's layman's terms. If I wrote 'Head of Pediatrics and Substance Abuse' then her parents might not understand. I would like them to be very clear about what the implications of this letter are."

Tenaya scribbles ink over the crest on her pack of Benson & Hedges. She presses it onto the top right-hand corner of the letter so that an inky coat of arms is left. She assures me that this has added to the letter's apparent authenticity. We pay for our tea and leave.

At home, Mum and Keith are sat around the kitchen table drinking coffee. I make a cup of tea and start to walk upstairs but Keith begins to talk.

"Hello, sport," he says. I believe that he has learned this name from watching American television. "Me and your mum were thinking about us all going on a holiday. What do you think?"

"Sounds nice."

(He is going to murder us both in a Third World country where the police force are corrupt and he can bribe them to "turn the other cheek.")

"How would you feel about Lanzarote?"

(Jesus said to "turn the other cheek." Jesus is Keith's partner in crime.)

"Ping went two years ago and he said it was nice."

(Lots of barren land, he said. Perfect for burying bodies.)

"You have the Psychology trip this weekend, don't you?" Mum asks.

"Yes, Friday and Saturday. It is in Plymouth. We are going to meet murderers."

"That sounds exciting," Keith says.

I have already met Keith, who is a murderer, and what I can tell you about murderers as ascertained from him is that they can blend in. Murderers can be social chameleons. You have to have a wealth of empirical evidence in order to get a conviction. This means that meeting murderers will probably not be particularly exciting because they will attempt to appear as normal, pro-social citizens.

"Yes," I say. "Very exciting."

I torrent a film noir on my computer then put the letter to Abby in a manila envelope. I got her address from the phone book because I know that her dad's name is Amadeus. When I take it to the post office, I wonder briefly what happens if front-desk postal employees are handed letters addressed to themselves. It is probably Royal Mail policy that they still put them into the system but I suspect that they secretly take them home. I do not think about it for very long because I am eager to go home and masturbate.

Inside of my room, the film noir has finished downloading. I do not watch it because, right now, my penis is a pent-up volcano or an old dam or a chubby cloud or a melting bar of Bounty.

I go to www.girlsoncam.com, enter my nickname as "Dr. Dong7" and begin a conversation with TghtYng-Pussy.

TghtYngPussy: hello
You: hi
TghtYngPussy: i don't want money

I feel affronted and flaccid. The girl looks young and is wearing a Mickey Mouse jumper. Her legs are bare.

You: okay
TghtYngPussy: what do you do?
You: i go to school

I am surprised by my own honesty.

TghtYngPussy: i used to go to school. i had to leave
You: why?
TghtYngPussy: money, we needed money. you can get money by putting things in your bum on the Internet
You: um
You: then shouldn't you be trying to elicit money from me?
TghtYngPussy: it doesn't matter. whether you pay or not, i will still have to spend every day in front of this computer

She lights a cigarette. Her eyes are like the eyes of an elderly cat.

TghtYngPussy: what would you like me to do?
You: i don't mind, it's up to you

TghtYngPussy removes her vermilion thong. This is an unprecedented first. Girls never remove their underwear in public chat. Then she just sits there, dragging on her cigarette, thighs parted like the Red Sea. I am Moses.

I pull one of Keith's golf socks over my penis. I have taken to using them in revenge. I am covertly avenging the death of Margaret Clamwell through guerrilla masturbation.

After four minutes the sock is full and I empty.

TghtYngPussy: are you finished?

You: yes, thank you

TghtYngPussy: it's okay. will you promise me something?

You: okay

TghtYngPussy: please work hard in school

She logs off.

This has been disorientating. In order to orientate myself, I write the draft of an e-mail that I will send when I can be sure that Amadeus Hall has read my letter.

<to: rainbowsandfireflies@hotmail.co.uk>

RE: Misfortune

Dear Abby,

I am writing to congratulate you on your recent acquisition, a fetus!

Kiera told me yesterday. I am sorry that your parents

grounded you and that you will not be able to attend either the Psychology trip on the 12th, or the cottage party on the 22nd. I'm sure there will be other parties when you are not pregnant, and they will be just as fun!

I would also like to confirm with you that the baby is not mine because we did not have sex. Although I did touch your vagina with my fingers, I feel 95% sure that they were free of semen and so the baby cannot be mine. Please do not tell anyone that I am the father of your baby! If you do, then we will go on Jeremy Kyle and do a DNA test and everyone will know you are a liar. You know what Jeremy thinks of liars. It would be a very humiliating experience for us both (but mainly for you).

You also have crabs, Abby! You gave them to me! I know this because I watched you scratching your groin when we were doing beer bong, which is why you dropped it and got beer all over your T-shirt. I tried shaving off my pubic hair and cleaning the infected area with bleach and wire wool but it did not work. After a brief consultation with Dr. Sarah Mathers, I was prescribed permethrin 1% cream, which comes highly recommended!

Abby, even though you gave me crabs and indirectly made me pubeless and will probably tell your friends that I impregnated you, I hope you have a good summer, and gestation.

Yours sincerely,
Jasper J. Wolf

The purpose of this e-mail is threefold: it will hopefully convince Abby of my innocence in regards to the letter; it will exempt me from fatherhood, should it turn out that I have impregnated Abby Hall; and it will make Abby think that she is not suffering the curse of crabs alone. Even though she is.

I think Abby Hall is suggestible so, like Julia, she will believe the things I tell her.

I decide not to show the e-mail to Tenaya because she will probably raise ethical objections to it.

8

It is 7:09 a.m. Mum is trying to wake me up using her hand. It is on my shoulder. I am irritated because today is Tuesday, the first real day of Study Leave, so I do not need to wake up at 7:09 a.m.

"No, Mum, it's Study Leave, I don't have to get up," I explain. I briefly consider using more aggressive dissuasive techniques (swearing).

"Yes, Jasper, you do."

"I definitely don't, Mum, please go away."

"The school called. Just sit up."

I sit up. There is sleep dust in my left eye. I only ever get sleep dust in my left eye. Dad used to call it "moon crumbs." Sometimes he caught so much of the moon in his sleep that he would be blind in the mornings.

"Did you know a girl called Tabitha Mowai, Jasper?" Mum asks.

"No, Mum, I did not know a girl called Tabitha Mowai. Am I now free to return to sleep?"

"The school phoned because they want everyone in this morning. There is going to be a memorial service for her. She hanged herself last night."

Mum does a thing sometimes where she lets me say insensitive things without me realizing that they are insensitive. She waits until I am done speaking to reveal why they are insensitive. I think she gets some secret enjoyment from it. Once, she let me talk for three minutes about how Keith's nephew didn't know anything about streets or gangs or drugs (not that I do) and so he shouldn't say anything about them. Then she told me that Keith's nephew had lost his brother in a gang fight and that he himself had sustained several bullet wounds, like 50 Cent, or Eminem.

I wish Mum would marry Eminem. He would rap about how much he loves me. *Me and this gun, we'll always be there for you, son.* Very nice.

She leaves my bedroom without saying anything else. This way I am left quietly alone with my own festering sense of insensitivity.

I decide to phone Tenaya in order to elicit details about the incident.

"Hello?" I say.

"Hi. Have the school rung you?"

Her voice is wet.

"Yes. Why are you crying? Did you know her?"

"No, but it's sad."

"People die every day. It's on the television. You don't cry every day."

"This is different. She was from our school."

"But you didn't know her. You didn't even know what she looked like."

Tenaya sighs.

"Why did she do it?" I ask.

"You know why she did it!" I begin to worry that I may in some way be implicated. "She was the baseball-bat girl."

I feel relieved because I did not have anything to do with the baseball-bat girl. Scott Jeppersen was the boy responsible for her humiliating rise to fame two weeks ago. She was somehow convinced to find an interesting use for a baseball bat, live on webcam. Of course, Scott Jeppersen, the lone audience member, decided to make use of his video phone. I saw the video because Jonah had it on his phone. It was just grainy porn featuring an abnormally young girl without real breasts. Not that the breasts in porn are real.

"But that was ages ago."

"No one shut up about it. Someone filled her locker with baseball bats."

"Did they? That must have been expensive." Tenaya doesn't reply. "How did she do it?"

"She hung herself with Scott Jeppersen's rugby sock, in her garage."

"That's interesting. Is a rugby sock long enough to fit around a neck and up a rafter?"

"I'll see you later, Jasper, good-bye."

She hangs up.

I put on my school trousers and sit on the bed.

It is strange thinking about how easy it is to end yourself. It is maybe the biggest decision possible to make and it takes so little effort. You do not need to fill out forms or save money or do a course at a local college. To cross imaginary lines drawn over the planet, you need to do more. You need passports and visas and money. But if you want to die, you can just tie a rugby sock around your neck and be gone forever. And your body will be taken to a crematorium where Uncle Eb will make screaming sounds and Mum will pass out and they will play Leonard Cohen as you turn to ash.

Scott Jeppersen must be choking on guilt. He is a sort of murderer, but it is worse for him than it was for Keith because he didn't mean to do it. Scott Jeppersen did not prepare to murder Tabitha Mowai and so he will not be able to blend in like Keith. He will not have read any books about how to do a murder and then act as though you haven't done a murder. Also, everyone will know that he murdered her and nobody knows that Keith murdered Margaret Clamwell. Except me, and Tenaya. Although Tenaya only counts as fifty percent knowing because she isn't entirely convinced.

Scott is sort of the murderer but everybody who watched the video and thought that it was both very funny and also quite disgusting was an accomplice to the murder. If nobody had watched the video and passed it around then Tabitha Mowai would still be alive probably and I would still be sleeping and Tenaya would not be crying. Tabitha also played a large role, however. Her downfall was brought about by her own tragic flaw: immodesty. In Shakespeare this is called hamartia. Tabitha's hamartia was necessary for her fate but it alone would not have been sufficient.

I take my trousers and boxer shorts off and walk across the landing to go for a shower. Keith sees me.

"Bloody hell, mate, put some clothes on."

I grin at him.

"Sorry, Keith."

He grins at me, too. He is probably a pedophile as well as a murderer.

In the shower I can feel the water dancing on my skin and I know that I am alive. And Tabitha Mowai isn't alive, even though she could have been. Her parents will say she should have been, but there is no such thing as should. I feel sad for her family and also jealous of her. I am not jealous that she is dead, I am jealous that her curiosity about death has been satisfied. Or has it? I don't really know. I think when people kill themselves, it isn't just to escape overwhelming emotional strain. People just let their curiosity about death grow until it is far taller than their overwhelming emotional strain. They probably experience mild excitement straight before they die. Like before you open Christmas presents, or before you have sex with someone you have not had sex with before.

I wrap a towel around my waist when I leave the bathroom, in case Keith has been hiding in a doorway with his camera. Then I roll a cigarette and leave for school.

It is not unusual for me to skip eating in the morning. Breakfast is the least important meal of the day for people who smoke.

The school looks particularly unattractive before the memorial, as though it's mourning along with all the crying kids who had laughed right through the video a few weeks earlier. The unwashed panes of glass seem to have dressed up in yet more dirt to show respect and the plastic wood floors are shining like sad eyes. Everyone everywhere is silent. Like completely silent, with their heads down and hands in laps. I do not think anyone really understands.

Teachers say that people (mainly girls and homosexuals) get particularly emotional when anyone dies because it reminds them of loved ones they have "lost." I think people get emotional because it makes them remember that they are going to die one day, which is something people forget very easily. Eventually, this leads people to resort to the rather cavalier philosophy of living each day as though it's their last. They always forget again after a day or something. In the West, people think that getting drunk is the most fun you can have; this is why it is the activity of choice at wakes. I think sex is more exciting, so if I ever attend a wake I will probably attempt to "pick up" a girl. This will prove easy because the girls will be vulnerable. I will feel only slightly guilty after I cum on their drunk and teary faces.

I am sat next to Tenaya in the hall, on the uncomfortable blue plastic chairs that all link together in rows as though they are reluctantly holding hands. She is not wearing any makeup and, although I can tell, it doesn't really make a difference. She is still fairly pretty. Still about an 8.5. I am a 7.

Scott Jeppersen comes in. He is crying into a handkerchief that obscures most of his face. As a murderer, he will have to get used to concealing his identity.

"Poor Scott," Tenaya says.

"What? You called him a dick last week."

"He is a dick, but he has a girl's death on his conscience now."

"Well, if you are going to share videos of a girl masturbating with sporting goods"—Ana Korsakov shoots me an angry look—"then you can hardly think that the girl will relish the attention."

"Yes, but I don't think he wanted her to die."

"Manslaughter, then. Five years. She's still dead, and it's still partly his fault."

Someone coughs. The Head has ascended the stage, wearing his pinstriped suit and familiar red tie (Mr. Hutchinson is a Labour man; some of the other teachers make jokes about this). He is holding a wad of yellow cards with notes on them. I wonder what they say. Probably just the key facts; these are:

— Tabitha Mowai, Afro-Caribbean origin, free school meals.
— Baseball bat masturbation, YouTube.
— Scott Jeppersen, murderer (not the sort that goes to prison).

There may also be some handy hints for the orator:

— Avoid words that could be seen as puns on baseball, e.g. "home run."
— Refer to Jeppersen as "the boyfriend" and not "the murderer."
— Do not blame the students, even though they are to blame.
— Attempt to sound genuine, as though the girl was well known to you. Use the relationship between Professor Dumbledore and Harry Potter as inspiration. Refer to her as "an active member of the school community."

Lots of people either cry or allow puddles to assemble along the ledges of their eyes. These people are statistically more likely to have not known the girl, or to have known the girl only through watching the video, than they are to have genuinely known her. This feels very strange to me. I do not understand occurrences like this. I think I am a broken human being. I am emotionally paraplegic and the entire school is playing football.

Because I am worried about my disability, I catch only certain buzzwords from Mr. Hutchinson's speech. These include "loved," "beautiful," "intelligent" and "full of life." Retrospectively, it seems that she was prime prefect material, except that she was not made a prefect because Mr. Hutchinson is making these things up. Her school report probably said "average."

After the assembly, some people go to the pub. Me and Tenaya do not want to go to the pub. Me and Tenaya go to her house. It is huge and Victorian, with ivy curling up the front like a pedophile's creepy fingers. Her parents had to take out a huge mortgage to buy it and as a result they have had to do the renovations themselves and switch from straight cigarettes to rolling tobacco. Her dad is plump and pink and her mum suffers from a disorder that means that she is really fucking weird. They both wear Crocs and smell of rosemary.

Sometimes her mum puts wine in the kettle. Sometimes she urinates in the garden and announces that she is encouraging the grass.

We are sat in her basement with a pot of tea between us. Steam is tentatively curling out of the spout, as though the air is an enemy castle. Tenaya has stopped crying but is looking down into her tea. I imagine touching her eyelids and feeling that they are still damp.

"I can't believe she's gone," she says.

I don't say anything. I do believe it because killing yourself is very easy. Even a dog could do it.

Mum had a talk with me about suicide once. I think this is because Mum sometimes experiences depressive mood swings and she is worried that they have been genetically passed down to me. The only trait I have inherited from my mother is cynicism. She told me, "Never kill yourself, it is a selfish thing to do." I told her it was selfish of her to ban suicide because at some point in my life I may be subject to unbearable physical or emotional pain. She looked upset so I placed my hand on her shoulder and told her that I am currently not experiencing unbearable physical or emotional pain. Mum said that she wasn't either.

I tell Tenaya that I do not want to talk about death because it is boring. I ask if she wants to play Scrabble, and she says yes, so I go to get the board from beneath her bed. Because of her mood Tenaya keeps spelling out macabre words like BLOOD and COFFIN and ROT, even though they are not what will get her the most points. I play BROKERING, she plays BYE, I play JUDGE, she plays JASPER. I tell her she can't use that. She asks me who I am and I tell her I don't know. I win.

Final scores:

Jasper 315

Tenaya 185

It starts raining and I tell Tenaya I am leaving. Outside,

the sky is concrete and the raindrops are ball bearings. They ring off the pavements and hide inside of my shoes. Rain smells of forests and it eats the familiarity of these streets. The wetter I get, the more aware I am. Aware that I am alive. And Tabitha Mowai is not. And Margaret Clamwell is not. My cheeks are tight and red. Tabitha's will be pale and papery. I wonder if dead people bruise when you punch them. I bite a ring of toothmarks into my forearm so it looks like a wristwatch. It hurts because I am alive, and this is all very disorientating, but I know I have a whole lot of things ahead of me, a whole life. And Tabitha Mowai does not. And that is even sadder than anorexia fetishes or pedophilia or people who cry because they feel guilty about watching porn videos of someone who has committed suicide.

9

I wake up at 10:20 a.m. The sun is already awake and has taken up residence in my room. Everything is very bright and warm, like a greenhouse. I open the windows and smell the air, which always smells of soil because our neighbor is an old woman who uses her garden as an allotment. Sometimes she gives Mum tomatoes. Mum says that she admires our neighbor for being proactive despite having lost her husband. She says that women can cope alone after they lose their husbands but men cannot cope after losing their wives. This happened to Mum's dad. When Gran died, his nails used to fill up with dirt and he would forget to shave or shower. Sometimes he would go without food for days so that he could save up enough money to visit this Vietnamese prostitute who reminded him of a girl from the war.

Mum is at work and Keith is sleeping because he has been working nights. I make tea and take a cigarette out onto the decking with the newspaper. The front page details the kidnap and murder of a young girl. The world has forgotten about Tabitha because the world moves on from everything. The world is a heartless murderer. It does not stop. Tabitha's parents have probably stopped. They will feel very guilty about everything for a long while to come. Every time Mrs. Mowai reaches for her Rampant Rabbit, she will see her daughter's face and drown beneath waves of guilt and sadness.

There is a picture in the newspaper of what the girl looked like before she was murdered. The girl had big, oak eyes. I realize that Keith must have murdered her because there probably aren't many murderers in this town. I write her name on my arm. It will be useful later.

I go back upstairs and turn on the computer. The carpet feels reassuring between my toes. Abby was not at the memorial so her parents must have received my letter and grounded her. This means that it is time to send the e-mail.

I click "send" and recline in my chair. Abby Hall is a Great Dane I feel disinclined to feed or exercise. I am experiencing "buyer's remorse."

Although I did glimpse Abby scratching her groin, I cannot be certain that she has pubic lice. I did not catch pubic lice from Abby and I did not shave my pubic hair or visit my GP. I felt guilty that Abby was experiencing so much misfortune and supposed that it might do her good to know that others were suffering.

Time for more tea. Tea contains theanine, which keeps you alert yet relaxed. I am reading this off the box of tea bags.

The doorbell whistles its melancholy drone as the kettle boils. Because neither Mum nor Keith are available, the responsibility of answering doors and telephones falls to me. Sometimes, when swimming in ponds of loneliness, this duty becomes therapeutic.

"Good morning. Have you accepted God into your life?"

I blink and stare at the man.

"This sounds serious," I say. "You had best come in."

The man is in his early thirties. He has cropped blond hair, combed tight against the contours of his skull. Two Bondi blue eyes and a well-fitted suit mean that my internal monologue is encouraging a trusting attitude.

He agrees to a sugarless tea and we adopt positions on adjacent sofas.

"Are you currently in a relationship with God?" the man asks.

He has a gentle, fluty voice. I feel like I can trust him. I hope he doesn't abuse my trust.

"I suffer from anxiety disorders, which means that maintaining stable relationships is difficult."

"Jehovah loves you, however you are."

He sips tea from my Harry Potter mug and passes over a copy of *The Watchtower*.

Jehovah's Witnesses believe that, following a cataclysmic end-time battle, 144,000 people will ascend to Heaven. They have dubbed this spiritual bourgeoisie the "little flock." Jehovah's Witnesses do not believe in Hell. These are the only facts about Jehovah's Witnesses that interest me.

Keith calls them "God-botherers."

"How many people do you believe will go to Heaven?" I say.

He looks at me, then into his gray tea, then back at me again.

"A select few."

"But how many *exactly*."

I am not being pedantic, I am probing.

"A hundred and forty-four thousand," he says.

I think he is ashamed. We observe each other.

"There are six-point-seven billion people in the world," I tell him. He nods. "That makes me feel sad. Would you like a cigarette?"

"We do not use tobacco."

Cults are so oppressive. Except for the Manson Family. They got to try lots of exciting things.

I tell him to wait one second and I pull out my phone. This is the calculation I do on my phone's calculator:

144,000 / 6,700,000,000 = 0.000021492537313432835

0.000021 x 100 = 0.0021

"Zero-point-zero-zero-two-one percent of people alive now will go to Heaven," I say, resting my hand on his leg, then feeling uneasy and removing it.

"I think I should leave," he answers.

"I understand."

I watch his lovely blond skull recede into the distance. What a brave man. It must be difficult to cope with the knowledge that there is a paradise but he is almost certainly not going to it.

In two days' time I will forget about him, like everyone forgot about Tabitha Mowai, like everyone forgets about everything, eventually.

10

When we congregated outside school this morning, Abby Hall was not there. This made me feel relieved and successful.

A fortune-teller in Brighton told me last year, "You will be successful in all of your endeavors." Perhaps this is beginning to be realized. Perhaps I will achieve four As and write a Booker winner and have sex with Georgia Treely. Except these things will not happen because I lack motivation, talent and charm.

We are sat on the bus. It smells of old women and travel sickness. Tenaya is reading Sylvia Plath and remaining stubbornly quiet. The air is chocolate. Everyone's mouths are occupied either with sexual gossip or salt-and-vinegar crisps. We are stationary but my stomach has already started to fester.

The bus driver introduces himself as Ben, attempts to win our favor with humor (What bus crossed the ocean? Columbus) and starts the engine. The engine sound, combined with the bus's drunken sway, forms a mild poison that turns my insides into a throbbing corduroy ache.

We are going on a Psychology trip to Plymouth. It is a "fun" optional trip that is our little treat for all the hard work that we will do during exams. It will involve staying in a hostel and attending a conference where a number of murderers and rapists will address us. They will likely attempt to include some sort of interesting twist so as to surprise and entertain us. I think I will feel bored and cynical, because we are listening to bad people who have done bad things and I would rather listen to good people who have done good things, although that is of less use in Psychology. Or the type of Psychology we do at school, anyway. They should give you the A-level options, positive and negative Psychology, because our Psychology largely involves learning about serial killers and schizophrenics but I would rather learn about people who are in love and kids who have beaten cancer.

Some of the girls will maybe find the murderers attractive. Ana Korsakov once remarked that Jeffrey Dahmer was "really fit" and "mysterious." He was an American man who killed seventeen people and attempted to turn them into sex zombies. Some of the girls may also find the rapists attractive because I know of at least three girls who fantasize about being raped. For example, when I had sex with Sarah Ivor she tried to make me choke her.

We will also visit a crime museum on the second day.

Mrs. Norton is reading the register in her furry whine. Even though she is not a Psychology teacher, she is coming because one of the Psychology teachers is attending his sister's civil partnership ceremony. The Psychology teacher that is not attending a gay wedding is called Mr. Mandalay, and today he looks particularly anxious. Mr. Mandalay enjoys folk music, rambling and evenings by the fire. I found this out one night when me and Tenaya were drunk and began to search our unmarried teachers on dating Web sites.

"Kimberley Acheman?" Mrs. Norton reads.

"Yes."

"Sarah Asti?"

"Yes."

"Imran Balki?"

"Yes, sir."

There is a small fountain of laughter. Mrs. Norton is deaf.

"James Falk?"

"Yes."

"Abby Hall?" A pregnant pause. "Abby?"

The girls sat along the back row fall into gigglefits.

"She's on maternity leave, miss."

Mrs. Norton mutters "Heathens!" then continues to read the register. I feel slightly guilty but the feeling is not overwhelming.

"It worked?" Tenaya asks.

"Apparently, yeah."

"Does she know you did it?"

"I extricated myself from the letter by sending her an e-mail about it. She hasn't replied. Her parents have probably banned her from using the computer."

"She will find out."

Tenaya leans back into her slim book with a sagacious turn of the head.

Abby Hall will definitely not find out. Even if she does, it won't matter. At present, I am only interested in short-term consequences. These are: an Abby-free trip and an Abby-free cottage. Room to carry out The Georgia Plan. I will deal with the long-term Abby-related consequences when they confront me. This kind of short-term thinking is called myopia. It is dangerous.

"Guess what?" Ping says, his face wedged between the two seats in front of us.

"What?" I ask.

In answer, he produces a surprisingly large press-to-seal sandwich bag of marijuana. I grin.

"The trip will be good," he tells me, turning back.

My indirectly drug-induced excitement wanes over the next two hours. Tenaya finishes her book and falls asleep on my shoulder. I roll a whole tin of cigarettes and one of the girls behind threatens to tell Mrs. Norton until Ping sits up and says, "What's that, Susie? Excess baggage?" (Ping went down on Susie Smith at a party last year and later described her vagina as "a ham Vienetta.") When Ping falls asleep, I use his phone to send *I'm hot for you* texts to his female cousins. I eat a Nutri-Grain cereal bar and also fall asleep out of boredom.

+

Urgh. Plymouth is a hideous concrete blitzkrieg. If it were a person, it would be the sort of person who eats the same thing every day and masturbates over pictures of steam trains. The buildings all seem to have been designed by a single manic-depressive town planner.

"Everyone line up," Mrs. Norton says. "The university is only a short walk away."

It is 11:47 a.m. Everything here is the color of boredom and surrender. It reminds me of my mum and Keith because they are an extremely resigned couple. They do not attempt to elevate themselves or their offspring (Keith's daughters both work as lap dancers in Birmingham) and seem perfectly content living in the smallest houses of the least-green suburbs and watching grainy repeats of *Holby City* every night. They are running on a treadmill that is not getting them into shape. Luckily, this failure of my mother's has not been bestowed upon me and I will continue to attempt betterment right up until I can afford to drink squash undiluted. This is the mark of a made man.

When we step off the bus, Tenaya says "Wonderful" as she takes in the scenery. Mrs. Norton beams. Ping then says "Jesus Christ," which obliterates the grin.

The only people I see while we walk have faces the color of dry clay. They only have eyes for the ground. The pavement. Our double-file walk is a funeral march.

When we reach the university, a short, shaky man with kind eyes takes us up to a long room with a projector screen. He smiles a lot, not just at the girls. We sit on the green plastic chairs to await further instruction.

"Shall we go now?" Ping says.

"I sort of want to see the rapist," I tell him.

"Why?"

"Deviant behavior is interesting."

"You're weird, man."

The rapist turns out to be a tall, thin man with skin like Blu-Tack and restless hands. When he speaks, the words bruise him. He makes me feel like a strong, well-rounded individual. I think this is part of the purpose of the trip.

"H-h-hello, my name is John and I did a bad thing and I am going to speak to you today about it and you can learn from me and help people when you grow up."

Tenaya is taking notes. She has written "Do not do a rape" in her exercise book.

"C-can anyone guess what I did?"

He jerks his head around. Several girls from other schools put their hands up. Ping also raises his arm.

The rapist is apparently unaware that there were timetables left on each of our chairs.

"Y-y-yes?" the rapist says to Ping.

"Pedo."

We all laugh. The boarding school girls throw disapproving stares. Mrs. Norton's jaw clenches and her eyes jump forward. The rapist eyes the ground.

"A-a-actually, no, I-I-I raped a—It was—"

"Did you rape a child? If you raped a child, then you still count as a pedo," Ping announces.

Mrs. Norton grabs him by his hood and leads him out of the room. Everyone is laughing. John the Rapist has forced his thin lips into a plastic smile. I feel a sense of mild amusement.

"That's sick!" someone shouts.

"N-n-no, I didn't rape a child."

A girl from the school seated to our left raises her hand. They are all wearing maroon blazers that have small trees emblazoned on their breast pockets. A surprisingly large percentage of them sport blonde pigtails that curl downwards like pouring bleach streams.

"Y-y-yes?" he says to the blazered arm.

"Why did you do it?" the girl says. "That's so horrible."

"Don't worry, nobody would bother with you," Jonah shouts.

There is more laughter. Laughter like hidden rocks revealed only as they emerge to trip public-speaking rapists. Mrs. Norton waves wildly for Jonah to leave, so me and Tenaya get up too and then we all stand around outside by the curb, looking blank.

"Where now?" Ping says.

"I don't know. That guy was fucking creepy," Jonah replies.

"We didn't get to meet the murderer," I say sadly. Even though I have already met Keith, I thought it might be useful research to see how he compares to other murderers. "I wanted to meet the murderer."

Before the trip, Mr. Mandalay gave us booklets entitled "Serial Killers: A Revision Guide." In them, he describes a theory called "The Triad of Sociopathy," which suggests that common childhood characteristics of killers are animal cruelty, an obsession with fire and persistent bed-wetting after the age of five. I have tried various ways of eliciting details about Keith's attitudes toward these things:

Animal Cruelty

At a family reunion last year, I kicked Grandma's dog Missy and whispered to Keith, "What a bag of shit, right, Keith?" He smiled at me. Because he enjoyed it. Because he is a murderer.

An Obsession with Fire

When Mum lights a fire in the living room, Keith gets angry and says she should have let him do it. He tries to hide his penchant for starting fires by claiming this is simply because "Women are shit at that stuff."

Bedwetting

This was difficult. In the end, I had to swallow my pride in the name of research. It tasted of dirt and old sick. When Keith came downstairs one morning, I took him aside for a man–to–semi-man chat. He enjoys these. I confided in him that I had wet the bed and asked whether this was normal for a boy of my age. He assured me that it was fine. Because he persistently wet the bed during his adolescence. Because he is a murderer.

We all light cigarettes then walk to a bar across from the university. It is called Ezee. There are echoes of soft jazz and silence ringing through. Jonah orders the beers because he is the only person who is eighteen, and we all sit around sipping them.

"What do you want to do tonight?" Ping says.

"We should stay in, then we can go out on the second night."

"Why do you want to stay in, blood?" Jonah has taken to referring to me as "blood" because, conveniently, it is both a lower-class colloquialism for "friend" and also a nod toward my drunken sex act. "Abby isn't even here."

"Yeah, why isn't she here?" Tenaya says, mocking, turning her head round to face me.

"She takes Psychology?" Ping asks.

"She sits by you," I say.

"Sorry, blood. I didn't notice because I was busy

learning while you were having staring competitions with her pussy."

Everyone laughs. Ping is not a learner. I am beginning to grow accustomed to these eruptions of laughter. I can't believe I had red sex with Abby Hall. I had red sex with Abby Hall. Abby Hall. Red sex.

When we have finished our expensive beers, Jonah goes to buy a crate of cheap beers and some vodka from one of the corner shops, then we wait outside the university. When she emerges, Mrs. Norton looks surprisingly stable and well, considering her earlier ordeal. She and Mr. Mandalay lead us to where we will be staying: Hope House Hotel.

"Good day," Mrs. Norton bids the receptionist. "We have a reservation for eighteen, it's under St. Mary's."

The receptionist punches some keyboard and rifles through some paper before delivering her conclusion.

"I'm sorry, I can't find anything."

"But we do!"

"I'm sorry, miss, I can't help you."

Mrs. Norton and the young receptionist eye each other for a while.

"Peter, do something," Mrs. Norton says. Her hands are swelling.

"I think we do," Mr. Mandalay whispers.

The receptionist's face fractures into a fat smile.

"Only joking!" she says. Mrs. Norton does not get on well with humor. "Welcome to Hope House Hotel!"

+

We are sat on the carpet in our eight-bed dormitory. Ana is lying with her head in Ping's denim lap and Jonah is sitting in his underwear, rolling cigarettes. He has very slim but defined calf muscles. That sounded gay.

A surprising fact about Jonah is that he is a devout Catholic, despite his promiscuity. Every time Jonah has sex, he bathes in cold water afterward to "cleanse himself." He says that this is the only reason he has not had outdoor sex. As a testament to his faith, Jonah let one of the boys from the year above tattoo the Virgin Mary onto his back using a tattoo machine he bought off eBay for a fiver. The boy only had black ink, so it's just an outline. Sometimes, when flirting, Jonah lets girls color it in with felt-tip pens.

"What's the plan?" Jonah says.

"I don't want to go out," I tell him.

"Does anyone have cups?"

"Yes, I bought fucking loads of cups."

Jonah takes the bottle of vodka out of its plastic carrier bag. We swig from it. Ana declines. It is a match down the grit length of my throat.

"I don't like vodka," Ping says.

"No one likes vodka, you dick," Jonah says. "That's the point."

We open beers and use them to soothe the burn. Ana's

fingers are playing over the top of Ping's hand. Jonah plays music on his iPhone.

Tenaya tells me she wants to go out for cigarettes so we follow the concrete stairs down and outside the hostel's plywood doors. The convivial receptionist is also stood outside, drawing carefully on a Richmond. Ping says Richmonds are the worst kind of cigarettes. He says they are potent at making men impotent.

She draws in a very somber way. It is the only somber part of her. It is a part of her that manifests only while smoking. It is strange to see a large aspect of a person given away only through small gestures, like when Keith uses homicide clichés or when Mum winks at my friends. People can never guard their embarrassments enough.

"Hi," the receptionist says. "Are you from the school?"

"No," I say.

We walk away and finish our cigarettes inside an uncomfortable bush, because talking to people who smile a lot is even more tiring than doing triathlons.

11

It is 8:45 a.m. My head is a junk band. Jonah just tried to wake up Ping by pulling his duvet off and when he did Ana was underneath it naked, curled around Ping's coffee-colored buttocks like a half-sexy leech. Ping swore and Jonah laughed.

"Breakfast time," Jonah announces. Today he is wearing a white sleeveless vest and very tight black jeans. His hair is a nest composed of old wax, haunted by the ghost of a pillow.

We all go down to the canteen, which is like the school cafeteria except full of homeless-looking people and backpackers. It is a "continental buffet breakfast." Tenaya has a croissant and I have jam on toast. Some of the old men get angry at Jonah because he drank the whole bottle of milk that was meant for coffee and is denying it, despite the white smudges of guilt around his mouth.

We arrange ourselves along the length of one of the tables. Unshaven men are burning Jonah with their eyes. We may have to fight our way out. Ana keeps trying to hold Ping's hand but Ping is trying to eat. The result is a sort of unacknowledged battle. They are at war but both acting as though they are not, like when a girl is kissing your neck and you have to subtly try to subtly push her head down so that she will suck you off.

"I had the weirdest dream last night," Ana says.

I stop listening.

+

We are in the crime museum. We have been here for two hours already. I have seen countless antique truncheons and torture devices and pistols and slave memorabilia. Earlier, Jonah took one of the Ku Klux Klan hoods off its display stand, put it on, and ran up to Imran, screaming, "Your end is nigh!" Imran punched him through the hood and Mrs. Norton almost fainted. Now Jonah has a swelling field of mold around his left eye.

Me and Tenaya are looking at an old electric chair from America. It has the nickname "Yellow Mama." Its informative plaque reads:

Early Electric Chair

First invented by Alfred P. Southwick in 1887 as a method of execution to replace hanging. His inspiration came from seeing a drunken man quickly die after touching exposed power lines. It is still in use in America.

"I can't believe they still use that," Tenaya says.

I shrug. "I can," I say.

Next to the chair is a clumsy model of Auschwitz inside a cuboid glass atmosphere. None of the exhibits are grouped logically. Next to Auschwitz is one of the splurge guns from *Bugsy Malone*. The whole building smells of cats and wet paper.

"Auschwitz," Tenaya says. She says it very quietly.

I know she is thinking the same thing as me. She is thinking about the History trip when we visited it. When we all sat in a semicircle of plastic chairs and listened to a survivor slowly recount his experiences. He looked as frail as a spun-sugar cage and had the blurred ghost of a number across his left forearm. Mr. Glover cried. Tenaya squeezed my hand until it didn't feel like my hand anymore. Jonah experienced something not unlike the opposite of a religious experience.

Mostly people wander around the museum touching things with their hands and noses. This often happens in life. Last year we went to the Tate and everyone tried to look as though they were interested in the art but actually all they wanted to do was touch it. People spent hours groping the marble sculptures. One thing I have learned from being alive for seventeen years is that people like to touch things very much.

Things that people like to touch:

Vaginas
Expensive things in shops
Jelly that is not ready to eat yet
Cigarette lighters
Necks
Dead things
Dogs
Glass
Scars
Piercings
Things that are on the floor but shouldn't be
Toddlers' cheeks
Snow
Each other's knees
Buttons
Bottoms

People also like to touch death. They do this by abseiling or by watching reports about Israel on the news. Touching is about curiosity. Curiosity is about death.

Once we have seen everything, Jonah insists that we visit the gift shop. The gift shop sells yellow rubbers and pencil sharpeners and large, brightly painted pebbles. Everything says PLYMOUTH CRIME MUSEUM on it. In one corner of the room an elderly woman is sat behind a gray plastic till, reading a Maeve Binchy and massaging her temples with slow, steady finger-orbits.

"This stuff is so shit," Jonah says. He throws a plastic letter opener back onto its pile.

The elderly woman winces. She does not look up.

"Can we go?" I say.

Jonah does not answer.

He walks over to a wire stand laden with novelty items. Itching powder, black soap, piss-flavored boiled sweets. Novelty items are the worst kind of items. Jonah enjoys novelty items. They make him feel as though he is sharing an in-joke with the rest of the world.

"Look at this," Jonah says, pressing a small packet into my hands. He is laughing hysterically. I turn the packet over. There is a picture of a crucifix and it says CATHOLIC CONDOM on it. Jonah has bent himself in half. He is laughing even harder. "It's a . . ." More laughs. "It's a . . ." Laughter. "It's a condom with the end cut off." He thinks that this is very funny.

"I do not think that is very funny," I say. "I think that it is highly irresponsible."

We walk back out to the main room where Mrs. Norton is stood, flapping her arms about, trying to count heads.

"Everyone!" Mrs. Norton says. She is stood beside an early policeman's uniform. "Myself and Mr. Mandalay will be leaving now. You may stay as long as you like, or return to the hostel, or visit the town. BE WARNED that curfew is SIX O'CLOCK, and anyone breaching that WILL face SEVERE PUNISHMENT."

Everyone nods and shuffles off. Ping and Ana disappear together, their arms looped like Olympic rings.

"What now?" Jonah says, removing a pouch of tobacco from his back pocket.

"I might go back to the hostel," Tenaya replies. She is still wearing the ghost of Tom. Time is the only suitable exorcist.

We both nod and Tenaya pats my arm then leaves.

"You are not going anywhere," Jonah tells me.

"Fine," I say. I wanted to do something anyway.

"What time is it?"

I pull out my phone.

"Five."

"Good," he says. "We are going to go and have some coffee now. Then I have a surprise for us. After the surprise we will get beers and go with the night."

"'Go with the night,' what does that mean?"

"It means that the surprise will make plans for us."

"The surprise isn't a hooker, is it?"

"Fuck off, am I paying for a whore for you."

We walk out into Plymouth's dull gray stomach.

12

"Mephedrone?"

"Yeah."

Jonah is grinning.

Mephedrone. The surprise was mephedrone. Mephedrone is a legal drug you can buy off the Internet. It is sold as "plant fertilizer." It lends you the kindness of the Dalai Lama and the charisma of Hitler, and all it asks in return is that, afterward, you spend a little while in a moody black hole.

"I don't know," I say. "Really?"

I am currently not emotionally equipped to deal with severe fluctuations in mood.

"Don't be a Gaylord." Jonah nods toward the toilet door.

We are in the kind of Formica café frequented by builders and people on benefits. All of the waitresses are from Poland or somewhere. Nobody's eyes even flick up when we both pass through the toilet doors.

There is barely any room in the cubicle. There are piss puddles on the floor with cardboard toilet-roll cores crumpled inside of them like aborted fetuses.

Jonah unfolds the powder, concealed in a wrap made from a leaflet for "An Evening of Delirious Dubstep." He uses his library card to make four lines on the toilet seat and we hoover them up.

We slouch onto the floor. Both sat with backs to tiles, we stare at other tiles for a few minutes. Burning nostrils, throat like a fecal waterfall, then I can feel it growing in my head.

My head is simmering.

"You okay?" I say.

"Yeah. More?"

"Word."

"Word?"

"What? I heard it in a rap."

Jonah smiles and shakes his head. He scrapes another two lines out of the wrap then licks the side of his library card. We take them and sit back. I feel huge.

"Thanks," I say.

"It's okay."

"Thanks, really. Not in like a gay way or anything, but I love you, man. You have great calves."

"I know, we don't say it enough. I love you, too, man. We're so young. Everything is good," Jonah says.

His hand is on my arm.

I put my hand on his shoulder.

"Yes, YES. People don't love each other enough. People love war and money. I don't love war and money. I love you."

"Yeah, fuck war and money."

"War and money can suck my dick."

"I love you and Tenaya and Ping and Ana."

"Ping and Ana! They are so happy together. They are wonderful. They are tiny stars."

"They'll get married and we'll all be there."

"Yeah, telling them how fucking sweet they are."

"All existing happy."

"Fuck war and money!"

"Weddings, that's what we should be doing."

"We should all get married."

"Confetti!"

Our legs are all bending about like blades of grass in a hurricane.

We push back through the doors and out into the café. We beam at the foreign waitresses then move toward the door. Jonah pushes it.

"Excuse, excuse!" the waitress says. "You no pay!"

She is beautiful. She is like a porn star or a *Vogue* model or something. She has huge cheekbones and huge eyes and I am very glad she exists.

"We are SO sorry," Jonah says. "Please, please forgive us."

He pulls a twenty-pound note out of his pocket and forces it into her hand. I pull out a ten and do the same. Thirty pounds for two coffees.

"Very generous," she says, returning our sloppy smiles.

"You are so beautiful," I say.

Me and Jonah both descend on her, pulling her tiny body into a fierce three-way hug.

"Please be happy," I say. "You deserve to be happy."

Outside the air is beautiful. It smells of potpourri. We drink it like drowning men. It fills us up full of sun.

"Let's find a club, spread some love."

"Right," I say. "People need to know we love them."

"Yeah, we need to scream it and hug them."

It is 8:00 p.m. Probably no clubs are open. We walk, anyway. Just following streets.

Jonah lights a cigarette. "Fucking beautiful," he says.

He passes me one.

"Uh," I say.

We pass a Tesco Express, an unbranded shoe shop, a soap shop, a Starbucks and a Debenhams. They are all wonderful. An alleyway opens to our left. Its walls are splattered with lurid splashes of neon paint.

"Down there," Jonah says.

We both skip through the alley. A sign looms, tacked to the red brick building ahead.

FUNKYTOWN: THE HOME OF DISCO

"Fuck!" Jonah says. "I fucking love disco."

"Fuck, disco, yes."

With that settled, we both go in. There are no bouncers guarding the doors because a seventies disco is not the sort of place that underage kids go to. It is the sort of place that middle-aged women and slightly-over-middle-aged men go to.

Funkytown is beautiful. There is music as grateful as school hymns ringing off the disco ball. The disco ball is beautiful. It is like what one of God's eyes must look like. The wallpaper is a scrolling collage of bright color and the floor is a wooden mirror. Pairs of people are dancing and smiling. They are happy. I am happy for them. There are people in flocks at the bar and in twos around the room. Sipping drinks and being humans. I want to tell them "Congratulations!"

"Congratulations!" I say. Jonah hugs me.

"Let's get drinks," he says. "Let's get drinks for ourselves and also for these VERY PRETTY WOMEN."

He says it very loud so they can hear. They need to hear because they are beautiful. They should be told. We are going to tell them. Tell them and buy them drinks and make sure that they are as happy as monks in a strip bar. Everyone is a human being!

There are two women. Both in their late thirties, maybe. They are beautiful shards of sun. One has blonde hair, as straight as my dick while I stare at her. She is wearing a tight polka dot dress and a polished scarlet belt to cinch in her waist. She must watch Gok Wan. There are lines around her eyes like picture frames. She is beautiful. The other one has short chestnut hair and is wearing a white summer dress. She is beautiful.

"What is it you're drinking then, ladies?" Jonah says. They tell him what they're drinking and he orders them drinks. I am totally occupied feeling brilliant and loving, so I do not notice really. He pushes a beer into my hand and ruffles my hair. "How's your night going then, girls?"

The blonde one grins. "Lovely, thanks, and you boys?"

"Oh, it was okay. Just got a whole lot better, though," Jonah says.

The brunette one laughs. "Want to dance, cutie?" she says, stretching out her hand. He takes it and they saunter off to the dance floor. I am very happy for them.

Now it is just me and the blonde one. She is beautiful. In films she could play Cleopatra, Helen of Troy, Keira Knightley or Reese Witherspoon. She smells of concentrated flowers and clouds. Her head is a marble bust of the sun.

"Not a dancer, then?" she asks.

"Oh, me? What? No, we can dance if you like. We can do whatever you like. What would make you happy? Let's do what would make you happy."

"Awwh," she makes a noise like she's looking at baby photos. "You're so sweet."

"Thank you," I say. "People aren't nice enough. People only care about money and, uh, and boats and castles and stuff. I don't care about that. Are you happy?"

"Yes." She is nodding her head.

"Do you want to dance?"

"I'm happy here. We can dance if you want to."

"No way," I say. "Finish that drink, I'll get us more."

I order more drinks from the barman. He is wearing a cowboy shirt and looks vaguely Mexican. I am delighted to meet him. I tip him five pounds. When I give it to him, I say "Share the wealth" and he laughs.

"So," the blonde one says, "what do you do?"

As propelled by "plant fertilizer" as I am, I recognize that in this situation honesty will only lead me down a cul-de-sac where I do not end up having sex.

"I am a police officer," I say. "And Jonah is a porn baron." I think he will enjoy being that. "We are both twenty-two but I am by far the more mature."

The blonde one laughs. She has teeth like pieces of chewing gum pressed together in their packet. Her lips are the color of watermelon guts.

"And what do you do?" I say.

"I'm a receptionist for an insurance firm, and Susie over there's a waitress, and don't try to ask my age." She winks.

It's like we're characters in a happy film. I am chatting up a beautiful woman in a bar and she will fall in love with me and our love will blossom like a sunflower in an eternal summer. Thank you, Jesus.

When his legs get tired, Jonah comes over and nudges me into accompanying him to the toilet.

"Why do you need to go to the bog together?" the brunette one says.

"I need a wingman," Jonah tells her. "Never shit alone."

Really we go to the toilet so we can fill our noses/throats/heads with more mephedrone. There is a lot left. No danger of tumbling down any hills yet.

"We are definitely going to pork those gash," Jonah says. "Fuck, they are so wonderful. This is perfect."

"Fucking beautiful," I say.

We leave the toilet.

At the bar, our catches have reconstructed the Great Wall of China using shots of black Sambuca. Black Sambuca is beautiful.

Jonah wraps his arms around the brunette one from behind and kisses her cheek. She grins. I grin at the blonde one.

"Ready?" she says.

"Four each," the brunette one says. "Last one has to make out with the barman."

Everyone laughs. I am happy. We are all existing and interacting. Well done, us.

Jonah is the first to finish. The blonde one is the last to finish. We all have black stains around our lips and down our necks and fronts. Everyone is smiling. I am smiling. The blonde one licks the Sambuca stains off my neck. Her tongue feels like Abby Hall's face.

"Oi!" the brunette one says. "You're supposed to be getting on the barman, loser!"

The blonde one laughs. Jonah does the type of whistling where you put a finger into each corner of your mouth. Is it called a wolf whistle? He is good at it. I am happy.

The barman comes over because of Jonah's wolf whistle. The blonde one grabs his cowboy shirt in her thin hand, pulls him toward her and throws her face against him. Everyone is laughing. Jackson 5 is playing. I can hear people singing. Jonah sings. We all go to dance.

+

Funkytown shuts.

I have reached second base with the blonde one and have good reason to believe that Jonah reached third base with the brunette one. The good reason is that he held his fingers under my nose and said, "Smell those babies, mate." Then we hugged. I am happy.

We all move outside, where it is cold and the wind is enthusiastic. A girl in sequined hot pants is being sick into a bin and a boy with heavily gelled hair is holding her extensions out of her face. Jonah laughs. I give the blonde one my coat and she kisses me. She says "So sweet" when I do this.

"Right, back to ours then?" the brunette one says. We all agree and start walking.

Their house turns out to be a semi-detached slice of suburbia. Is the mephedrone wearing off? I say this to Jonah. He nods. When we get inside, we turn to go to the toilet but the brunette one says, "Whatever it is, you can just do it off the kitchen side." And the blonde one adds, "Just let us have some."

We let them have some. Jonah scratches out eight lines and we all suck them up. One of the girls puts on some music. I don't recognize it.

"It's Etta James," the brunette one says. We all hug.

"This is beautiful," I say.

"So beautiful," Jonah says. "You two are amazing."

"No, *you* two are amazing," the brunette one says.

We all hug.

The blonde one pulls me onto a sofa that smells of cheap wine. Behind it there is an upright piano. A dog idles into the room like a child who has wandered onto the stage of a play.

"This is Peter," the blonde one says.

"Hi, Peter."

"Hi, Peter."

Jonah and the brunette one disappear. The blonde one is kissing me on the sofa. She leans back and tugs at my collar until I am laid flat on top of her. I have never lain on top of breasts so experienced before. She guides my hand up her thigh. I guide it around the edge of her lace pants. Her vagina feels like a Brillo pad.

"Let's go upstairs," she says.

She takes my hand in hers and pulls me up the stairs. I stare at her beautiful ass the whole time, thinking about how happy I am.

I am going to have sex with her. It will be practice. I

want to be as good as possible for Georgia in Devon. I must work on my stamina.

Her bedroom is . . . I don't notice. We collapse under the duvet. My T-shirt falls off quickly, and my trousers, and my socks. We join forces when attempting to remove her dress but we are both unwilling to disentangle our lips so this proves difficult. Difficult but not impossible. I consider myself an expert at the removal of bras, that part is not a problem. Then we are both near naked. I am laid between her legs like a dot in Pac-Man's mouth. We are kissing. Her left hand blindly spanks the bedside table in search of a condom. A condom is found. She dresses me in it. I enter. Sighing. Moaning. I am a yo-yo. Turning her over. Slapping her ass and rocking backward and forward. Sighing. Moaning. Sleeping.

13

The comedown from mephedrone is my least favorite type of skiing. You begin to hate everyone around you. Like a pedophile in a nursing home. You want to be alone. Then you realize that you don't really want to be alone, you just want to stop existing. You want to keep folding in on yourself until you aren't there anymore. Which is how I feel now.

I can't find the time anywhere. It is still dark. I don't know where my phone is. I feel anxious when I don't know what the time is. My throat is an Arizona highway. I am lying next to the woman, staring at the back of her cheaply dyed hair and ballooning with regret. I really despise this woman, and this house. I despise Jonah, too, but I should find him.

Fuck, she probably has kids.

I'm totally naked. I can't find my boxer shorts but I do find my jeans. The denim is a cheese grater against my testicles. Fuck. Jesus, my head. Okay, Jasper J. Wolf, pull yourself together. Now is not the time for an existential 9/11. You must keep moving. Find clothes. Find Jonah. Leave.

The carpet annoys my toes. I walk out of the bedroom and across the landing into the bathroom. Jonah is in there, stood in the bath, with the shower raining over his head. His Virgin Mary tattoo is staring at me like a disabled person. Jonah is mumbling a prayer.

"Can you stop with that shit so we can leave?" I say.

He turns around. "Fuck off, how would you know anything about any God? You'll go to Hell."

I can still feel the residue of the mephedrone like a sea of india ink through my head. I hate Jonah. I want to disappear. Why are we walking, talking or moving?

"Please let's fucking get out of here," I say.

He turns off the shower and climbs out. "My head fucking kills."

I make sure to kick Peter in the ribs on the way out.

When we get back to the hostel, everyone else is happier than us. Or at least less ill. Ping and Ana are curled around each other, whispering, and Tenaya is reading on her bed.

"Where the fuck have you been?" Ping says.

Jonah falls onto his bed.

"Me and Jasper have made a pact never ever to talk about anything that happened last night ever again. As my friends, I will trust you will respect that pact and not attempt to elicit any information from us."

Tenaya laughs. "Ugly girls?"

"Worse," I say.

"Shut up!" Jonah wraps a pillow around his head and groans.

On the coach back home I fall asleep on Tenaya's shoulder while rain kisses the windows and Mrs. Norton reads out loud from her Bible.

PART 2

Exhumation and Fires

14

Mum and Keith are putting together an IKEA bookcase in the living room. It looks like a boat at the moment. Keith swears. Mum sighs. In the event of an apocalypse, they would both be fucked because they lack the practical skills that are required for survival in our dystopian future. A man capable of killing lions with his bare hands will probably shoot and skin them both. He will fashion their skins into a mackintosh.

I am sat in the kitchen with a German textbook, not revising. It is more exciting watching the two of them. Open-plan living is cheap cinema.

"Keith, where's 4C?" Mum says.

"There isn't a 4C, darling."

"But look."

She holds the instructions up to Keith's face. My mum

dislikes instructions. She calls them "destructions." This is a joke. People tell jokes when they do not know what else to do. A lot of jokes are told in hospitals. Usually, these types of jokes are not very good.

"It's wrong," Keith says. "The instructions are wrong."

Mum is appalled. "I'll phone IKEA," she says. "I'll complain."

Keith grins. "I don't *fore-see* you getting much help."

They both laugh. Keith can't even do puns well. I have no idea what Mum sees in him. Maybe he has a penis the size of a toddler.

"Excuse me," I say. "Hello. I'm Jasper. I'm your only son, and I'm trying to revise."

"Ooh," Mum says.

"We've been sent to the naughty step, love."

They kiss. It is disgusting. I go up to my room.

My phone is on my bed upstairs. It is vibrating. It is spinning itself in circles on my pillow like a Catherine wheel. Tenaya is calling.

"Jasper?" she says.

"My parents are trying to make furniture," I say. "Keith made a pun and they kissed. It's disgusting."

"I'm thinking about Tom."

"Still?"

"He was a big part of things for a long time, Jasper. No matter what you thought of him."

I breathe hard into my phone. "He was not a good boyfriend. He is an irritating human being."

"Jasper, you aren't helping."

"What is there to help with?"

"I don't know what to do."

"I've got like a half gram. I'll bring it over if you want."

"Argh."

Tenaya hangs up.

I do not know what I have done wrong. I did my best. I try. *You have to try to understand other people, Jasper. Imagine you are them.*

Tom was my boyfriend and now he is not. I loved Tom very much. Tom cheated on me. Tom left me. Tom has such nice cheekbones. Tom will probably become a rich art dealer. I don't know what to do now. Tom. I don't know what to do now. I loved him.

Julia: empathy

Tenaya: nicks on her arms

Radio: the mental state of self-harming adolescents may deteriorate if they do not get the help they so clearly ask for by harming themselves

Oh.

OH.

I run downstairs and hurl my body out of the front door. I shout a good-bye to Mum. I pelt down the streets. I am an advert for Nike footwear.

Up along our road, then a left at the Hungry Horse, past school, past a woman with a Monroe and an empty pram, past two men sipping cheap lager on a low wall, past the Baptist church and Happy Shopper and Ben McKay's house.

Tenaya's.

I throw my body over the fence at the end of her garden. Her parents are keeping chickens in case of an apocalypse. Tenaya's stood with her back to me on the other side of her kitchen's French doors. She's probably got a palmful of paracetamol. I have to stop her.

Things I can see near the French doors:

Spade

Pot plant

Bench

Plastic bucket

Plastic bucket is the only option. Not a dumbbell, not a feather. I pick it up and swing open the French doors. I bring the bucket down as hard as I can on her head. She screams. She whips round to face me. It didn't work. Should I try again?

"JASPERWHATTHEFUCK?"

"Um."

"What the fuck are you doing?"

I grab her wrists and squeeze them. Her hands open like flowers. She is not holding paracetamol.

"You said you were going to do suiciding," I say.

Tenaya blushes. "I didn't."

"You were thinking about it."

"I wasn't."

"I know you were. I've learned how to empathize."

"Shut up, Jasper."

She sits down on one of the kitchen stools. I stay standing.

"I don't know," she says.

"I was scared," I say. "Jonah's disgusting and Ping has Ana."

"Sometimes," she says. "I don't know."

"I don't either. But I told you to text when it happens. I'll buy that two-for-five-pounds wine from Imran's and we can watch *Labyrinth* in your bed and I'll let you pluck my eyebrows."

"I called."

"You didn't make it clear enough."

"Okay."

"I'm going to boil the kettle now," I say. This is something people say when they want to let someone know that everything's okay but they don't know how.

There is a stain on Tenaya's kitchen wall in the shape of a rabbit's head. It was born when Tenaya's mum threw a cup of coffee at Tenaya's dad. Nobody washed it off. They have stopped working on renovating the house.

"You said you were going to boil the kettle," Tenaya says.

"I just said that to—" She didn't understand. "Okay."

We take the tea up to her bedroom and watch old episodes of *Sex and the City* from beneath a duvet. Big does not deserve Carrie.

"Are we going to Twelve Cats tomorrow?" I say.

"I guess so."

"They're getting better."

"Will you go to Asda with me afterward?"

"Why?"

"I need to get food. Mum won't buy any. She just gets drunk and orders takeaway."

"Okay."

"Thanks."

"Ping said we could go over to his before."

"Mm."

Tenaya nods then falls asleep. I take a book off her bookshelf at random and sit on the window ledge, reading. The book is called *Women on Top*. It is about the different ways that people have sex in their heads.

15

7:38 p.m. Ping's band are playing at the Twelve Cats tonight. I am going to wear my wolf T-shirt. At gigs you can throw your body around and rub it against girls and they can't swear at you for it because everyone is just having a good time.

Ping's band are called Deep Emotional Skaing. He believes that puns are funny. Puns are for old people and bad poems. Last year they won a local competition and some of their songs got put on iTunes and they had a CD made. The CD was called *Fuck The Free World, Mary Jane*. This means nothing.

When I have dressed, I go downstairs and put my head in the fridge. Cold yellow light licks my face. There is an unopened bottle of blue-top milk in the fridge. I unscrew the lid and peel off the white thing. I stand up and glug milk.

Mum appears behind me.

"Jasper," she says, "stop that now. Other people have to use that milk."

"But, Mum, it's good luck to drink straight from a newly opened bottle."

"I don't care, Jasper, get a glass."

I drop the milk bottle back into the fridge.

"Mum," I say. "I'm going to see Ping's band tonight. Can I have some money?"

Mum frowns. "How much?"

"Ten big ones."

"Don't say 'big ones,' Jasper."

"Why?"

"It's what the Mafia say."

"Fine. Can I have ten pounds, please?"

Mum sighs and passes me a note from her purse. I grunt at her so that she knows how grateful I am. I go out to catch the bus.

+

Ping's mum answers the door. She is wearing a dressing gown. Her hair is wet. My penis is screaming in my pants. It is upset with me for not allowing it to climb into Ping's mum's vagina. She probably has a beautiful vagina. A perfectly shaven gorge.

"Hi, Jasper," she says. "They're upstairs. Go straight up."

"Thanks, Mrs. Lin."

I bound past her and up the stairs. Ping, Ana and Tenaya are all sat on the bed, laughing. Ping and Ana are holding hands. I wonder who will surrender first: Ping's penis, or Ana's virginity. Girls think that their virginities are priceless glass figurines. All they are really is three minutes of embarrassment followed by a sinking disappointment followed by the question, "What are you thinking?"

"What're you doing?" I say.

"I got a new phone," Ping says.

He holds it up. Looks like a fake BlackBerry. It doesn't seem funny.

"I don't understand the joke."

"Jonah told me about the Psychology trip."

I gulp. "Um. What?"

"You know."

"Prick."

Ana laughs. Frigid bitch. I look at Tenaya. She's looking at the duvet pattern.

"So he's about to find out he's got a little guy on the way."

I laugh. "Yes, yes."

"Who's going to speak?" Tenaya says.

"I'll do it," Ana says.

"You can't do it."

"Why not?"

"That stupid accent," I say.

"Leave her alone." Ping crosses his arms.

"Don't be gay."

"No," Tenaya says. "Just he knows your voice already."

"My sister's back from uni," Ping says. "I'll get her to do it."

"Will she?"

"Yeah, I used to phone school all the time pretending to be Dad when she didn't want to go in."

Ping leaves the room and comes back a few minutes later with his sister. She is a hulky female with a flat chest and a monobrow. She's wearing an Oxford Brookes T-shirt. It is difficult to believe that she came out of Ping's mum. I think the reason she didn't want to go into school much must have been because people called her Frida Kahlo and stabbed her with pens.

We say hellos and Ping briefs her on what to say. She nods. She doesn't say much in response but when Jonah picks up the phone she becomes an Oscar-winning actress.

This is all we hear:

"Jonah?"

"It's Susan, from Plymouth."

"I'm pregnant."

(We gag ourselves with our hands.)

"Yes, I'm sure."

"Well, I did a pregnancy test."

"No, they're pretty much always right."

"I don't know, ninety-nine-point-seven percent or something."

"Yes, but it's not a huge chance, is it?"

"Grow up, you're going to be a father."

(Ana chokes on a laugh.)

"Yes, I'm keeping it."

"Yes, you'll have to pay me money until it turns eighteen."

Ping tears the phone out of his sister's hand.

"Happy Father's Day!" he shouts, hanging up immediately to avoid Jonah's siege of *fucks* and *cunts* and *pricks*. We all fold over ourselves, laughing.

+

12:15 a.m. Me, Tenaya, Jonah and Ana are being thrown about by a crowd of sweating kids. Deep Emotional Skaing are playing on a low stage. Jonah bought some pills. He gave me one in the toilet. He said he didn't know what they were. I feel different. I feel okay. I feel warm. It sounds as though the band are playing one huge note without stopping. The note has grown huge and swallowed the room. We are all inside the note. It is our castle. A shirtless man's back collides with my face. My lips taste salt. Who am I supposed to be? Tenaya is bobbing up and down. Her hair is flying about her face. Ping is grimacing. His hands are clawing at his bass. Ryan Samuels is the singer. Ryan Samuels is screaming and his face has turned the color of a Gideon's Bible and it might explode and it might shower us all with bloody scraps of cheek. He launches himself off the stage. We raise our hands. I support his crotch. I squeeze. I am not gay. We pass him backward. He jumps down and steals someone's beer and runs back up onto the stage. Ryan Samuels empties the beer over his crowd. People scream. People want more beer. They start another song. Ping is on his knees. Ping thinks that he is very good. He is just playing one note. I am inside the note. This note is our new home, for now, which is forever.

+

When the band have finished playing, we go outside to smoke. Me and Tenaya sit at a damp picnic table. The pill is wearing off. I am only vibrating slightly now. People are stood in circles, talking loudly about the music. Ping is still backstage putting his stuff away. Ana runs out of the pub, holding a rum and Coke, and joins our table.

"Wasn't that so amazing?" she says.

"Great," I say.

Tenaya smiles. "So," she says, "you and Ping."

"He's wonderful," Ana says.

"He's Ping," I say. Love is a cult.

Tenaya gives me a look that means she thinks I am being a twat.

"But you're going back to Moscow next year?"

Ana grins. She is in love with Charles Manson. She will commit murders because he will tell her to. Nobody will understand why. The police will carry her away and she will not scream but her eyes will be the eyes of the last Bengal tiger left in Bhutan.

"I'm not," she says. "I'm staying. I'll get a job in a café or something. Me and Ping are going to live together. He's going to try and take the band all the way."

"All the way," I say. "Wow."

"Jasper," Tenaya whispers. She hits my leg under the table.

"I love him," Ana says.

Girls can be so gay. Even Tenaya is finding it hard keeping the laughter in her throat captive.

Ping emerges from through the back door. His face is flushed and he is wearing a crown of sweat. Ana runs to him and buries her face in his brine-soaked T-shirt. He kisses the top of her head. Me and Tenaya tell him that the band played great. We say that they are getting much better and that their new song sounded like it could be a radio hit. I make sure to use the phrase "all the way."

After a few minutes we excuse ourselves and go to catch the 96 to the retail park with Big Asda in it. It is only a short bus journey. Tenaya falls asleep on my shoulder. I nudge her awake when we reach our stop. She blinks as though she does not know where she is, then smiles.

Big Asda is open twenty-four hours a day, seven days a week. 1:21 a.m. It is the last torch left lit in the retail park. Huge sheets of light fall out of the windows and lie across the tarmac night like the bodies of naked angels.

Tenaya pulls a deep trolley out of its queue and we go through the automatic doors. My body temperature jumps. A security guard filling out a sudoku grid looks up. He does a small bow as we enter. He seems like a warm, well-mannered man. I wish that Mum had married him.

"What first?" I say.

Tenaya shrugs.

We walk through the refrigerator aisle. It is deserted. Tenaya puts a fat bottle of green-top milk into the trolley. I put a chocolate milkshake in. She takes it out and asks me if I am eight years old. She suggests I buy an Actimel instead. I tell her that I would rather give the money to a heroin addict.

In the dried-food aisle she lowers a huge bag of lentils into the trolley. I look at her with disgust. She goes on to add raisins, prunes and cashew nuts. It is too much. I lie prostrate in front of the trolley.

"What are you doing?" I shout up.

"What are *you* doing?" she says.

I stand up.

"We are two seventeen-year-old children alone in a supermarket and you are buying fucking prunes. You should be buying huge bags of chicken nuggets and Polish beers and cigarettes."

"Jasper," she says, "since my parents bought that fucking house all they have done is get drunk and order cheap takeaway. We eat takeaway for lunch and for tea, and then leftover takeaway for breakfast. I do not want any more shitty food."

That makes sense. "Fine."

"Go and get some chicken nuggets, though."

"Okay."

I sprint to the frozen section and pick up the largest bag of chicken nuggets I can find. Tenaya has moved on to browsing the vegetables when I find her again. She has added one iceberg lettuce, three leeks, four tomatoes and a red onion to our trolley.

"Done?" I say.

"Yeah, just need cigarettes."

"Will you cook chicken nuggets when we get back?"

"Yeah."

"And can we watch *Gilmore Girls*?"

"Fine."

16

I am bored. I have spent the day pretending to revise. Really I was playing 3D Pinball Space Cadet on the computer. Eventually I will reach the rank of Fleet Admiral. My perseverance will be rewarded.

6:30 p.m. I have eaten a filling dinner of sausages, mashed potato and onion gravy. I called Jonah and asked what he was doing. He told me he was doing nothing and said I should come over. I am leaving the house now.

"I'm going to Jonah's, Mum," I say. "Bye."

I shout this at the empty living room.

Mum appears from nowhere.

"Be very careful," she says. "Don't be back late."

"Yes, Mum."

"Ten, at the latest."

"Ten is ridiculous, Mum."

"Is it?"

"Yes, I will not be back later than eleven."

I slam the door behind me.

I have had the last word.

The 38 bus goes to Jonah's. It only takes seven minutes. I sit on one of the balding seats and watch the sky outside peel like old paint. There is a woman stood in the aisle by my seat. Her hand is curled tight around the pole. She is squeezing hard. All of the color has fled from her fingers and up into her modest breasts and sad-looking cheeks. Her nails have been bitten down to half-size and they are flecked with specks of red.

I do not understand people very well.

I will not eat my own fingers.

I will not hang myself with a rugby sock.

I will not murder my ex-wife by punching her nose bone up into her brain.

+

Jonah opens the door after I ring the bell six times. We go through to his living room and collapse on the sofa. He is watching the Disney cartoon version of Robin Hood. The one where Robin Hood is a fox.

"This bit is so good," Jonah says.

A small white rabbit wearing a large hat has just fired an arrow over a wall and into a game of badminton being played between a hen and a vixen.

"Yeah."

For reasons I do not yet understand, I always cry when I see other people crying on the television. This is why I do not watch *Secret Millionaire*. I can only hope that the future will tame the wild horses in my eyes. I still believe that the reason Samantha Black would not have sex with me last year was because I cried during *Juno* and she thought that I was gay.

I hope nobody cries.

The small rabbit does not look very happy.

"Jonah," Jonah's mum shouts from the kitchen. "Jonah, get out of the living room, I want to watch the news."

Jonah's mum has watched the news every day since her husband died in Afghanistan. She is just looking for someone to swear at. She swears indiscriminately. I have witnessed it often. She swears at Trevor McDonald, Hannah Montana and Gok Wan. She calls them all cunts.

"Let's go upstairs and play Xbox," Jonah says.

"Do we have to?"

"Yes. We can play Halo on Xbox Live."

Jonah knows that I like listening to angry people shouting on Xbox Live.

"Okay," I say.

Usually I do not like computer games because they are dull and bad for character development, however playing Halo on Xbox Live is good because you can converse with aggressive foreign people and then shoot them. Usually, behavior like this is not allowed.

In the first game that we play someone called BurgerThing424, who has a Northern accent and a shotgun, calls Jonah a noob and then laughs at him. Jonah calls the person a fucking Paki. I ask Jonah how he knows the person is a Paki and Jonah tells me he knows this because BurgerThing424 keeps shooting him in the back of the head. I do not really understand the joke.

Jonah goes up to the top of the water tower. He says he is going to snipe people from there. He tells me just to hide or ride around in the jeep or something. If I attempt to engage in the game, he says, our team will definitely lose. I nod. I only want to listen to the talking, anyway. I strut around the bunker, collecting useless weaponry and body armor.

"Got you, you Paki cunt," Jonah says, grinning.

"Stop being racist," I say.

"Don't be gay."

"And homophobic."

"I'm not scared of you."

To prove this Jonah throws a large explosive from the top of the water tower. Despite being safely in a bunker, my half of the split screen shivers. Jonah chuckles.

"This is shit," I say.

"What? Did you see that?"

"Oh?" I say. "You mean that small collection of pixels that just shifted around on your television screen while the voice of an unemployed Mancunian man shouting 'Fuck you' invaded your bedroom?"

"Don't be a prick."

"I am not being a prick, this is just boring."

"Fine, let's finish this one, then we can go out for a joint."

"Okay."

Our team gradually accrues points. Jonah remains on his viewpoint, picking off members of the other team while they continue to re-spawn and hurry around the virtual environment.

Eventually I get bored and begin running wildly through the most exposed areas.

I die many times.

"What the fuck are you doing?" Jonah says.

"I am seizing life by the horns," I say.

He drops the controller and sighs.

"Let's go outside."

Outside, our breath makes ghost jellyfish in the air. Marijuana smoke claws at my insides. I relax. We sit on the edge of his decking, our feet wetting themselves on the damp grass.

"Jonah," I say, "have you thought about what you're going to do once school is over?"

He shrugs.

"Still got another year to think about that."

"But you must have some idea."

He crushes the joint out with a grinding motion in the grass by his foot. He lights a normal cigarette and passes me one.

"The army," he says. "I think the army."

I light my cigarette. My body feels tense. I am trying not to be loud and insensitive.

"The army," I repeat.

"I know what you think of it, don't bother."

"Okay."

"What about you?"

I try to alter my body language so that it looks less negative.

"I am going to be an award-winning novelist," I say. "I am going to buy a house on the Costa del Sol. I am going to sleep all day and fuck all night."

Jonah laughs.

"Can I visit?"

"Yes," I say. "Yes, you can."

Back in the house we watch *X Factor* from Jonah's bed. I do not say anything. Jonah often interrupts with comments.

Things Jonah says while we watch *X Factor*:

Man, she should win, she's so fit.

Seriously, man, she'd get it.

Is he gay, or what?

He is gay.

Everyone votes for the gays.

I bet Mum votes for him.

Do you reckon I could go on this?

I reckon I could win, you know.

Then he sings that song from *The Lion King*.

I tell him I'm leaving.

"Fine," he says. "See you, man."

I like Jonah a lot. I hope he does not join the army. He could be a young Russell Brand.

Outside, I can see no stars. The only lights in the black are the things that we have put there: streetlights, house lights, blinking planes. I feel as though I am intruding on a large piece of conceptual art. I am leaving tiny, muddy footprints.

While I am stood waiting for the bus, two boys pull up beside me on bikes. They press only the front brakes so that the bikes come to a stop after long, arced skids. The boys have scarves pulled up to their eye lines. They both have hoods up: one blue, one black. I am extremely scared.

"All right, mate," blue hood says.

"Yes, mate," I say.

It is important to speak how you are spoken to in situations like these.

"Give uz ya phone, mate," black hood says.

He smells of body odor and wet dog.

I do not move.

I am in a state of shock.

"Givuz ya fucken phone," he says again.

I am not worried about being punched. I am worried about pissing in my pants.

"Givusyafuckenphonenow," he says. A single long compound word. It will never catch on.

I fidget in my pocket. I pull off the back of my phone and pluck out the SIM card. At home, I will put the SIM card into my old Nokia 3210 and everything will continue as normal. That will show them.

I hand over the phone.

"Andyawallet," blue hood says.

I think about pulling out my penis and spraying them both with piss.

"I do not own a wallet."

Neon-yellow acid piss that will make them both permanently blind.

"Whyzat?"

Cunts.

"Uh."

Black hood pushes me.

"Go on, fuckoff."

I begin to walk defeatedly off into the night. My heart is a snare drum.

One of the boys throws a rock and it catches the back of my head. I press my hand to it and it comes away red. I wonder if I am going to die by stones.

And another.

This time my neck.

They are the Taliban, I am a woman falsely accused of adultery.

I run.

Back at home, in the warm light of my room, I sit in front of the computer. I swivel my head. My neck hurts.

I do not know what to do. I decide not to tell Mum. If I do, then she will become extremely scared for my safety and will not allow me to leave the house without either an armed guard or a large and grumpy mastiff.

I know what to do.

Sometimes, when I feel sad or ill, I play the old Avril Lavigne album and think about how happy I was in 2003, when kissing a girl who tasted of Panda Pops at a school disco was enough to make everything seem as though it couldn't get any better.

I am listening to that Avril Lavigne album now. I am mouthing lyrics to the ceiling. If Mum saw this, she would be scared that I was gay. I am not gay. I am young, and a bit scared.

17

I am sat at the kitchen table across from Mum. We both have cups of tea; hers has two spoons of sugarless sugar-substitute, mine has four. Sunday. She is wearing her Lycra trousers and smelling of sweat because she has spent the morning at the gym. I have not told her about the brutal assault that took place last night. I have only just woken up. My hair is a fistful of straw. It is 11:15 a.m.

"Jasper," Mum says, "I hope you realize that these exams are extremely important."

"Yes, Mum."

"And it is very important that you use Study Leave to study."

"Very important," I say, nodding.

"Perhaps even important enough to consider waking up before midday?"

"It's only eleven, Mum."

"Nonetheless, Jasper, when I was studying for my O-levels, I woke up at seven o'clock every day to get enough revision in."

"I don't want to be a . . . whatever it is you are."

Mum sighs. "You are too young to know what you want."

Keith comes down the stairs in his dressing gown, rubbing his eye and scratching his genitals. His gray hair is stuck up at funny angles and his yellow toenails are plodding. Definitely a murderer.

"Morning, champ," he says.

Sometimes I wonder how he manages to come up with a new name every single time he sees me. He must watch *Friends* every day and take extensive notes. I imagine that the inside of his wardrobe is filled with Post-it notes that offer suggestions for friendly names to use each day. One day I will follow him around for ages and see if I can exhaust his supply.

"See," I say, "Keith only just got up as well."

"Keith doesn't have important exams coming up."

"Give the kid a break, honey, it's hardly life or death," Keith says. I don't know why he does that to himself. He ruffles my hair. There is blood on his hands, metaphorically.

I place my hands on the table. Mum looks down at them, then up at me. She screws her face into an unattractive shape. She knows that I am going to ask for something.

"Mum," I say, tilting my head slightly to one side to remind her that I am a wonderfully adorable and charming son, "if my exam scores are above the national average, can I get my nose pierced?" Nipple was probably too much. Nose is reasonable.

Mum allows her face to fall. She does not believe that this is a serious issue.

"No, Jasper," she says. "No, you cannot."

"The key to a successful mother–son relationship is compromise," I say. "I will work hard at school if you promise to give me the personal liberties I deserve."

Mum pulls her mouth to one side. I do not know what is happening inside of her head. Mum has a simple mind. It cannot hold many thoughts.

She turns to Keith.

He grins.

She turns back to me.

"Okay," she says, "here's the deal. You can get one earlobe pierced if your exam scores are above the school's average."

Mum has tunneled under my plan! She knows that the school's averages are higher than the national averages.

"Earlobes are gay," I say. "Eyebrow?"

"Ear."

"Lip?"

"Ear."

"A dermal implant above my left collarbone?"

"Ear."

"Belly button?"

"It's the earlobe or nothing, Jasper, that's the deal."

I exhale. I wish she would stop saying "deal." My mum thinks that she is Noel Edmonds.

"My penis, then?"

"Don't be disgusting," Mum says. "One day you will thank me for stopping you from mutilating your own body."

"It isn't disgusting, Mum. Actually, it's very sensual. It heightens the sexual experience for both partners. You are so closed-minded."

Keith nudges Mum and makes a sexual sound. Mum ignores him. She leans in close to me. She is Julia.

"Jasper," she says quietly, shifting her teacup to one side as though she is scared I might hide behind it, "are you sexually active?"

What a tricky situation. I decide to use a trick that I have learned from Julia. Leaning back, I glance at my wrist, even though there is no watch on it.

"Ooh," I say, "look's like time's up. Sorry, Mum."

I go upstairs.

I lie on my bed and try not to think about the blonde mother. It is difficult because my imagination fills the room up with a crowd of people screaming "You did WHAT?," and I have no answer for them. I play Los Campesinos! on the laptop. I erase my head with a pillow.

The phone rings.

"Jasper?" It's Tenaya.

"Yes."

"What are you doing tonight?"

I stand up, look around and scratch my groin. "Nothing, I guess. Why?"

"Can I come over?"

"Sure."

She must be tired of sitting alone with Tom's ghost. She must have realized that real company is better than ugly stains on happy memories.

"Thanks. Is six okay?"

"Sure."

"See you later."

"Bye."

I sit on my blue swivel chair (Keith stole it from his office skip) and pull myself up to the fake-wood desk. A Psychology textbook is already open, sprawled like a naked woman in front of me. Actually, no, not like a naked woman at all; it's a thousand times less seductive. If it were a naked woman then I would be learning her body with my eyes and running my hand over my dick like it's a tube of toothpaste with not much left in. But it is not. It is something about autism and how to detect it. I don't want to be an autism detective. I want to go to sleep.

+

Tenaya arrives at 5:30 p.m. She is wearing a white summer dress and old boots. She looks pretty again and she is smiling. In the kitchen I boil the kettle and she sits on the marble top, swinging her legs.

"How is thinking about Tom?" I say.

"I think I'm over him."

"You do?"

"Yes. I think getting over something isn't forgetting it but learning to live with the memory of it."

"Uh-huh."

She laughs. "Like how you managed to cope without Abby."

"Losing Abby was hard," I say. "I went through many sleepless nights and hours spent weeping into my cupped hands."

"Did she ever find out it was you?"

"Not sure."

"I'm guessing she had some suspicions."

We take our cups of tea upstairs and lie on the bed. I play Feist on the laptop.

"We are exhuming Margaret Clamwell tomorrow," Tenaya says.

"Shit, yeah," I say. I had completely forgotten. "I think Keith has some balaclavas somewhere, we can wear those."

"You really want to wear a balaclava?"

"Yeah, why not?"

"Well, doesn't it seem a bit criminal?"

"I don't know, maybe. But as soon as we get the body, everyone will know that Keith is the criminal and not us. We will be heroes."

"And what if there isn't a body?"

"There definitely is a body."

"If you're sure."

"I am sure."

+

When I wake up the only light in the room is a thin beam shooting out of the DVD player's display panel. The television screen has switched to standby. Tenaya is sleeping bent into herself like a horseshoe on the right side of the bed, her dress still on and bunched in pockets around her back.

I go downstairs and eat four Weetabix with four tablespoons of sugar and half a pint of milk. The kitchen clock says 6:30 a.m. but the kitchen clock is always ten minutes fast. Ten minutes fast, but not fast enough to outwit me. I have learned its little trick. As a clock, it has little else to do but try to pull its feeble jokes on people who actually have places to be. I have a place to be. I have to save my mother's life.

"Here," I say, licking Tenaya's forehead to wake her up. I pass her a cup of tea. "Rise and shine." We both sit on the end of the bed, sipping the teas, staring at the wallpaper.

"If there is a body . . . ," Tenaya says. She doesn't finish.

"Shh," I say. "We will just pull the head out of the ground and then phone the police."

"You can be the one who touches the head."

"Okay, I will touch the head."

My phone vibrates. A text from Ping. *U coming tnite?* I look at Tenaya.

"Did you want to go up the hill tonight?" I ask her.

"I don't know. Not really."

"Okay."

I text back, *cnt sry, busy*. Then I look at the time on my phone (6:40 a.m.) and add, *y u up?* After a second Ping texts back, *hvnt slpt yt*.

When Tenaya has finished her tea, I get the balaclavas and we quietly leave. Outside it is a typical bright suburban morning. It is not a very long walk and the only people we see on the way are an overweight man in a polo shirt who is walking a pit bull the color of conkers, and a blonde MILF jogging in Lycra with a serious and motivated expression on her face. Tenaya scolds me for following the progress of the woman's buttocks with my eyes. She says that the woman is not an object. I say that I know the woman is not an object, but her anus is.

18

Before the exhumation I drew a penis on back of Tenaya's balaclava in Tipp-Ex so that, if we were seen, people would report a penis balaclava to the police and they would find it in Tenaya's possession and she would be arrested and I would go free. Unfortunately, she noticed before she put it on and insisted we swap, so now I am exhuming Keith's ex-wife with a crude white phallus drawn on the back of my head.

We have been digging for around half an hour at the suspicious mound using only our hands. Tenaya hasn't been doing much because she doesn't want dirt in her nails. I told her that this is a matter of life or death but she didn't believe me. The sun is full up and the sky over our heads is clear blue, as clear as the skin on Georgia Treely's cheeks. In order to brace myself for the horror that waits, I have been picturing Georgia Treely winking at me in a yellow bikini. The family who live at the house will wake up soon. We still haven't found anything.

"I think we should go," Tenaya says.

"Do you want my mum to die?"

"I don't think your mum is going to die, Jasper."

"People didn't think Martin Luther King was going to die, either," I explain. Tenaya sighs hard.

I keep scooping dirt up with my hands. All I find is a Pog with a picture of Taz the Tasmanian Devil on it. I put the Pog in my pocket and keep digging, my hands turning the color of chow mein. After a couple of minutes Tenaya pulls me down onto the dirt so we are both laid flat on our stomachs.

"What the fuck did you do that for?" I ask.

"I saw someone move in the house."

"Then why didn't we run? How is lying in their garden going to help?"

I notice that a small pebble is pushing against my crotch and I move my hand down to pull it away.

"Jasper, what are you doing?"

A girl dressed in pajamas covered with small cartoon elephants steps out of the house into the garden. She doesn't see us straightaway. The pebble is still pushing against my penis and left testicle. The girl removes a cigarette from behind her ear and lights it. The girl sees us.

Tenaya is the first to stand up. She removes her balaclava. I leave mine on.

"Thank you for not screaming," Tenaya says.

"What the fuck are you doing?" the girl says, quieter than expected. The cigarette stays in her hand, fast turning to a cylinder of ash. Neither of us say anything. My groin hurts so I rearrange my penis with my hand through my trousers. "Can you stop touching your cock, please?" the girl says. "And take off that fucking balaclava."

I take off the fucking balaclava.

"Sorry," Tenaya says. "We were looking for our cat."

"With balaclavas?"

"Human faces scare Rupert." The girl stares at us. "We are going to leave now."

The girl nods. Her face is red. Her face is an exploded can of tomato soup.

Me and Tenaya turn, run and vault back over the fence at the end of the garden. We run until we are three streets away and then we stop to pant. I roll and light a cigarette. Tenaya takes my tobacco and does the same. We sit on a low brick wall.

"Rupert is a shit name for a cat," I say.

"It was a better excuse than rubbing your dick."

A bald-headed man hand in hand with his small ginger son passes us with a funny look spread across his face like an ugly oriental fan.

"Do you think she'll tell her parents?" I ask.

"No." Tenaya shakes her head. "She woke up early and went outside to smoke. It would be easier to say nothing than to try and explain that."

Once we have regained our breath and finished our cigarettes, we walk back to my house for breakfast. Mum and Keith have already left for work so we do not have to make excuses. We sit at the kitchen table with bowls of Cheerios and mugs of tea. I use my Harry Potter mug and Tenaya uses Mum's BEST MUM IN THE WORLD mug. I did not buy the mug for my mum. Keith bought it and wrapped it up and gave it to me to give to her on her birthday. He did this because he knows that I am selfish but he does not want Mum to know this because it will make her unhappy, and if she is unhappy she will maybe leave him and he will not get to murder her. He does not want to miss out on murdering her. For Keith, murder is even better than anal sex.

"It didn't work," Tenaya says.

"Yeah," I say. A stream of milk runs down my chin, swallowing the small hairs like poverty-stricken children in a tsunami. "I feel bad."

"We should revise."

I do not want to leave Tenaya alone, especially after a failed exhumation, especially in the company of text-books. "We could go to the party tonight." Her arms will thank me.

"No, we need to revise."

"Do you remember last time we went up the hill?"

Tenaya laughs.

The last time we went up the hill was back when we enjoyed setting things on fire. We would wander around the emptiest suburbs, looking for old sheds and houses. Both of us were excited when we found the shed on the hill. It was locked so we just stuffed newspaper balls in its gaps and cracks then lit them with matches and sat back toasting with beers.

It is exciting watching the shed dissolve into tangerine plumes that flood the dappled green forest light. I can see the reflected orange in Tenaya's eyes. The fire warms the glass of our beer bottles.

Then screaming.

And scratching.

A very desperate scratching, coming from inside the shed.

A man runs out of the building. It is difficult to examine him because parts of his body are on fire, like his trousers and hair for example. His mouth is open. I can see that his teeth are small ivory stubs, laced with black pits and yellow scabs, like the heroin addicts Mrs. Thorne used to play DVDs of in PSHE.

"Fuck!" Tenaya screams. I feel a surge of gratitude that she has not adopted her mother's penchant for the beautification of curse words. "Fucking do something, Jasper."

I look at Tenaya and then at the ground and then at the burning man, who is now very close to us and rolling around like a long, thin cheese without a hill. I look at Tenaya. I look at the man. I should do something. I feel scared and apprehensive because the man might try to stab me with one of his needles, which could cause me to contract HIV which could in turn cause AIDS which could in turn cause death. I look at the building. I look at Tenaya.

"WHAT THE FUCK?!" she screams, staring at me expectantly. I always let people down. I am very selfish.

I stand over the man, clutching my small, shriveled penis and showering him with urine until he kicks my shin hard, which makes me want to kick him back. I kick him back. My instinctive act of retaliation is followed immediately by a swell of guilt because he is still on fire and I am not. His eyes are bigger than any eyes I have ever seen before.

I keep pissing because, as Mum says, he will thank me one day.

"You were lucky he didn't punch you in the dick," Tenaya says.

I pick up our mugs and carry them over to the sink.

"Yeah," I say. "So we're going to the party?"

Tenaya sighs again. She sighs often. "Fine."

I am the savior of adolescent arms.

I leave a Post-it note on the fridge.

Not back tonight, Mum. Have fun.
With love,
your favorite son
(Jasper)

19

4:06 p.m. We are stood outside Ping's house, knocking on the white plastic door. His mum answers. She is wearing a Led Zeppelin T-shirt and her lips are painted the color of pink glow sticks. Ping's mum is extremely sexually attractive. I consider winking at her. I decide not to wink.

We ask if Ping is in and she tells us he's in bed and we can just go straight up. As we walk past, I make sure to graze her nipple with my shoulder. I apologize and she smiles. I would like to have sex with her very much. If Ping's mum were a prostitute then I would commit credit card fraud in order to raise enough money to buy sex with her.

Upstairs, we file into Ping's bedroom and begin jumping on his sleeping body and making loud, meaningless sounds. We continue this until he starts shouting "Fuck off" and slapping our grinning faces. Eventually he pulls himself into a sitting position on the bed.

"What time is it?" he says. His voice is blurry from sleep.

"Four."

"Four?" he repeats. "Then what the fuck did you wake me up for?"

After saying this he tugs the duvet back over his head. Me and Tenaya punch him through it until he sits up again.

"We have to go get Jonah," Tenaya says. "Then get up the hill."

"It still won't take that long."

"Jonah doesn't want to drive in the dark again."

Ping laughs.

"Such a pussy," he says, shifting out of bed. He stands up beside us in his boxer shorts and scratches his head. "Okay," he says. "Okay."

We watch while he finds jeans, a T-shirt and a hoodie, then we all go downstairs. Ping takes a slice of toast out of his mother's hand, kisses her cheek and we leave.

The walk to Jonah's isn't long but Ping uses it to try out several new Abby Hall jokes he seems to have come up with.

"Hey, Jasper, what was it like fucking a girl with Stonehenge for a face?" he says as we turn onto Jonah's road. Even Tenaya laughs.

Jonah's parents are at work so he lets us in. We join

him sitting on the sofa, watching *Celebrity Big Brother*. We try to guess who the celebrities are. I tell Ping his mum is fit enough to be a celebrity and he punches my arm. Tenaya asks if the black guy is Will Smith. Ping calls her racist.

"You want beers?" Jonah asks.

We all tell him we do and he goes out to the kitchen. When he comes back we all sit sipping from cans, staring at the television. We all sit staring at other people sat staring at each other.

"I wish George Bush would go on *Big Brother*," Ping says.

"George Bush wouldn't go on *Big Brother*," Tenaya says.

"Why not?"

"Someone would shoot him."

"Didn't someone shoot him already?" Jonah asks.

"No," I say. "I'm quite sure George Bush is still alive."

"You'd think someone would have shot him, though. Americans are supposed to be fucking crazy and all they talked about was how much they hated him."

"Nobody's shot Obama, either," says Ping.

"Everyone loves Obama."

"Because he's black. It's not cool to be racist anymore."

I think of my Klan T-shirt and Julia. I must remember to bring up Obama with Julia. Keith called him an uppity wog once.

"Can we stop talking about America?" Tenaya says.

"You know Ana's little sister?"

"Yeah."

"She's spent so much time watching American TV, she has an American accent."

My mouth contorts. "That's fucked."

"Yeah."

"Hannah Montana's fit, though."

"Yeah, she is."

After *Big Brother* all that's on is a repeat of a *Friends* episode that we have all seen six times, so we leave.

We have to go pick up Ana. It's not far. When we get to her street, she's stood in the road shouting at an old woman in a yellow hat. The old woman has a face full of folds and moles and her eyelids are half-closed.

"The house is that way," she shouts. "You stupid fucking woman, go back, stop following me." Ana is mean.

Ping explains that this woman is Ana's grandmother and also her sole legal guardian. This makes Ana a Nankid.

In the car Ana tells us that her grandfather died six years ago and that sometimes her grandmother puts on his old glasses and just sits crying into them. I tell her what my mum said about women being able to cope when their husbands die. Ana says that's a stupid thing to say.

It's a half-hour drive up to the clearing on top of the hill and we have to stop off on the way to pick up alcohol and cigarettes. By the time we reach it, the sky is dark and Jonah is pissed off.

20

In the clearing on the hill a healthy bonfire is burning. Beside it, someone has hung a plank of wood from a tree with frayed blue string, making a swing. A tall girl I have never seen before is sat on it with her eyes closed and dribble down her chin. Ketamine. Three tents have already been pitched and most kids are sat on blankets or logs in congregations around the fire. A boy from the year below is sat by a bag of firewood, hurling blocks into the flames. Crystal Castles is playing out of a portable iPod speaker.

We greet the people we know and check out the ones we don't. There are a reasonable amount of attractive girls. Georgia Treely is not there but I did not expect her to be. She would not be allowed to go and she would not have much interest in going. She is probably at home, revising with a decidedly unwet vagina and Mahler on low in the background. Georgia Treely likes Mahler very much. Georgia Treely does not like Sam because in business studies once he said that climate change isn't happening.

We drink beers until everyone decides that they are drunk enough and then we just sit. After a while Jonah turns to me with a confused look across his face.

"Jasper," he says, "what generation are we?"

I shrug.

"I don't know. I think, like, Z."

"No, it's Y," Ping says.

"I thought we were Generation X."

"No, you dick," I say. "Generation X was like Van Halen and shit."

"I think we should be Generation Bum."

"Why the fuck should we be Generation Bum?"

"Because we're the first generation to have cast off the stigma attached to anal sex."

"No, we aren't."

"Yeah, I'm not going near anyone's ass."

"Fine, then we're Generation Twat."

"You're Generation Twat."

"Whatever the generation is, I don't think we're much part of it."

"What? Why?"

"Exactly what percentage of the world's population do you think are middle-class white kids?"

"It's the rich kids that make the generation, you idiot, of course we are."

"Yeah, otherwise Generation X wouldn't have been named after a punk band. It would have been like Generation Malaria or something."

"Generation X wasn't named after the band, it was named after that book."

"No, it wasn't, that book was fucking gash. It's named after the band."

"My mum says we're the Facebook Generation," Ping says.

"Argh, I would love to fuck your mum."

Ping raises his middle finger.

Everyone laughs.

An hour later and Jonah is explaining about this thing they do in Eastern Europe for midsummer. He says that they build bonfires and take turns jumping over them, and each time someone jumps over they throw on more wood. He says we should try it. We are all drunk. We agree.

Jonah says that he will work out the order using the random number generator on his phone. I sit next to him. Really he just writes down the order he thinks will be funniest. It goes like this:

Jonah
Me
Ping

Tenaya
Ana

He grins at me then reads out the order. Ping protests Ana's placement but Jonah tells him that God has spoken.

Me and Jonah jump the fire easy. Before Ping goes to jump, Jonah empties the entire bag of firewood onto the fire. The kids from Baccant High are staring at us. Ping pushes Jonah. They are going to start arguing but then someone runs in between them, madly twitching.

"FUCKFUCKFUCKING HELP ME," he shouts. "WATER. BEER. ANYTHING COLD. HELP. FUCK."

"What the fuck's wrong?" Tenaya says.

"NETTLESFUCKINGNETTLES. FELLORWAS-PUSHED INTO THEM. FUCKING HELP. HELP."

His face looks like tiger bread. I like tiger bread. There are long red mountain ranges across his skin.

Jonah throws an empty beer can at his head. He staggers away, trying to shake off the sting.

Tenaya tuts.

"Shouldn't we have helped?"

"No," Jonah says. "That kid's a twat."

"You didn't know him."

"I could tell by his face. Anyway, if he wasn't a twat then why would someone push him into nettles?"

"Because they were a twat?"

"You're a twat."

21

When the sky is full black, Tenaya sits staring at her hands in the light of the fire. This means her head is probably clouding. She needs to move. I ask her if she wants to walk. She nods very quietly and we both get up. Everyone else is drunk and in conversation or falls of laughter so we are not noticed.

We walk up out of the clearing. The only light is the light from the bonfire. It slips in streaks between the tree trunks. We follow the patterns it makes across the dirt and leaves. When they soften and drop away, I pull my phone out of my pocket and use that as a torch. We walk upwards some more then turn left until we come out at the steep sloped field with the lightning-blacked oak tree. From the tree's low branches we can sit and see all the streetlights and bright windows below. I smoke and Tenaya swings her legs. She kicks her shoes off her feet and into the tall grass.

"Tom has a girlfriend," Tenaya says.

She pulls a small bottle of supermarket vodka out of her coat pocket and sips it. She passes it across to me. It tastes of hospitals. I pass it back and we sit quiet for a while.

"Who is it?" I ask.

"Lydia Jenkins."

"The one in the year above with nine fingers?"

Tenaya laughs.

"No, the one in the year below who always wears a bandana tied across her head."

"Oh," I say. "Her."

"I'm not over him really," she says.

"I know," I tell her.

She passes the vodka back across and turns her head toward me. One of the windows turns black. Several others light. I turn to face Tenaya. Her eyelids are low and the sleeves of her coat are pulled down over her knuckles.

"Soon, we will be old and I will have a bowler hat and you will have a Labrador," I say. "You won't remember his face."

"From up here we can see everything," she says. "But we aren't here yet."

We pass the vodka back and forth for some time, watching the lights below and wondering which ones will one day be ours. I roll us both cigarettes and we sit blowing smoke rings into the harsh air. After a while Tenaya says that she is cold and asks if we can go. She says we can walk. It will take hours but I agree and I take out my phone to use as a torch as we trip back through the trees toward the main road.

The road down the hill is steep and awkward and full of potholes. We stop every now and again to make cigarettes and lie down on our backs. Stood in the road, Tenaya takes my hand and says, "I don't know."

A car coming down the hill makes sounds like an old asthmatic man. It pulls to a stop beside us. The car is an old Citroën with a curved bonnet and headlights on stalks. A man's head leans out of the open window. The head has white cloud hair with a small skullcap resting over it.

"Sup?" the head says. "Where you kids goin?"

Tenaya looks at me and I nod. We know we should not get into cars like this but we are drunk and also the car smells of pot, which means the man will not be very fast-moving so we can run away if he tries to kill or rape us. Tenaya tells the head her address.

"Sweet," the head says. "Get in."

I have to sit in the front passenger seat because one of the back seats has a car engine on it. Once we are in the car, the man lights a joint and begins to drive. He drives silently for a few minutes then turns away from the road and toward me.

"Wha's your name?" he asks.

"Jasper," I say.

"You ever had a bar mitzvah, Jaz?"

"Jasper," I say. "And no. My parents are Christian."

"You had a lucky escape. Sitting there reading that fat bitch of a book in front o' all them kids. You trip up and your parents give you the 'fuck?' eye. S'like you been caught wanking inta that sock all over 'gain. Fucking hell. Don't ever agree to have a bar mitzvah. Not that I had a choice."

"Shit," I say. Tenaya vomits giggles from the back. The Jew doesn't notice.

"Yeah, shit. Being a Jew sucks."

He draws on his joint. His fingers twitch. The Jew isn't watching the road, he is watching his hands. The car swerves gently and the front left wheel catches the curb, jolting the car. In the mirror I can see Tenaya's mouth open. The Jew jumps and lifts his head back up. He stays silent again for a while.

"I'm no Jew. Not fo' real. You know what I am?" I shake my head. "I'm a disciple of pussy."

I don't say anything. Tenaya laughs harder.

"You ever read the Bible, Jaz?"

"No."

"I read the Torah. I read the Bible. I read the Qur'an. Don't read any of 'em, y'ear?"

"Yeah."

"They all just God's word after a thousand years of Chinese whispers. Bent-ass Chinese whispers. You ever play Chinese whispers at school, Jaz?"

"Sure, a few times."

"The teacher always starts it wit like a real normal sentence, ya know? Then there's a few kids who hear it perfect good from the kid next to 'em but they think it'll be fuck funny to change it up. Throw in a 'fuck' or a 'dick' or a 'shit' or a 'bitch,' right?"

"Yeah, I remember."

"The kids do it to boost their cool. 'Yo, you know the kid who dropped the N-bomb into circle time, man, that kid's hot shit.'"

I nod fervently. He passes me the joint.

"That's the Bible, Jazzy. It's not God's word. It's God's word with a few 'fucks' and 'dicks' and 'shits' slipped in. Except the Bible don't say 'fuck' or 'dick' or 'shit' in. You know what it says?"

I don't answer. I'm chewing the thick air. Marijuana smoke drifts in tiny clouds between our heads.

"It says, 'Women, cover yo' heads an' gays burn in Hell an' don't you dare use them fucking condoms, kids, an' what you doin' working the Sabbath, Mum?'"

He watches the ceiling a while. I join him. The ceiling. There are wide brown rings drawn from his cigarettes, stamped into the plaster like the stains of giant teacups. We watch them until the car swerves again.

The Jew gestures for me to hold the wheel while he rolls another joint and lights it. I hear him whisper to himself, "Smoke it like iss yo' woman.

"Hey, Jazzy."

"Yuh."

"You want to know what God's word really was?"

"Yuh."

"He say, 'Fuck that bitch in the pussyhole, yo.'"

When we reach Tenaya's house we say thank you to the Jew and he mumbles "No bar mitzvah," then passes me a joint. He shakes Tenaya's hand and then tries to kiss her but she pulls away. His eyes don't change shape. He is used to being pushed back, I think.

We go straight down to the basement of Tenaya's house and she boils the kettle for tea. Her mum is sat at the table with a bottle of red wine. There are red smudges around her mouth and stains down her blouse in close splotches, like an archipelago after years of war.

She tells Tenaya that her father is a cuntbucket.

She tells me that I am a good kid.

In bed me and Tenaya arrange ourselves with our spines pressed against each other. They don't match well but it feels good. Before falling asleep she tells me that *Waldeinsamkeit* is the German word for the feeling of being alone in a wood.

22

The walls of this room are the color of petrol. There is a boy in the corner wearing a wooden necklace and stroking the hair of a girl without a face. Green numbers are scrolling over the floor.

"You want to be careful of those," says the boy.

"Why?"

"The Matrix," he says. "The fucking Matrix."

I pick a vase up off the floor and throw it at the wall. It smashes. The pieces scatter across the room.

"Watch it," the boy says.

I take a candlestick off the mantelpiece and throw it at the boy. It catches his head. Blood runs down his forehead, along the valleys either side of his nose, into the corners of his mouth.

"You're fucking mental," he says. He takes the girl's

hand and pulls her into the fireplace. They run into the black.

"No," I shout. "Stop it."

I take framed pictures of nothing off the coffee table and throw them into the fireplace. They shrink then disappear. I pull off my trousers and throw them into the fireplace. I throw my jumper and T-shirt and socks in after them.

"No," I say. I curl into a ball on the carpet. "No."

There is a black balaclava on the window ledge. A crucifix has been painted onto the back of it. I can see it from my ball. I stand up and pull it on.

I leave the house.

Jonah is in the garden. A field of wheat. A salmon-pink sun the width of the world. He's chopping wood blocks with an axe the size of his arm. There is a half-built log cabin behind him. He does not stop when I approach.

"What the fuck is that thing?" he says.

"What thing?"

"That thing on your head."

I run my hands up over my head.

"It's a metaphor," I say. "It shows how I can be surrounded by people and still feel alone and anonymous."

A block of wood splits in two. The halves fly away from each other like wrong-way-round magnets.

"Take it off," Jonah says. "You look like a prick. And go back inside. If you stay out here much longer, I'll have to build you a coffin."

"I don't like it in the house."

"Then get up from the living room floor."

I turn around and go back inside. The walls of this room are the color of tulips. The floor of this room is Astroturf.

In the kitchen, Tenaya climbs out of an oven. She crawls to my feet and stands up. Her face is close to mine.

"Take it off, Jasper," she says.

"No."

"Take it off."

"No."

She grabs the balaclava with both hands and pulls. I throw my right hand into her jaw. It cracks. She falls back onto the lino. Half her face is red with blood. She is a bear that has been messily gorging itself on fish. She has a fit like an epileptic. Her lips are stretched so wide they meet her chin and nose.

"What are you doing?" she says.

"I'm participating in a dream scene," I shout. "For my novel. My novel. It will give readers an insight into my inner feelings. It will make the book longer."

"What are you doing, Jasper?"

"A dream scene," I shout.

"What are you doing?"

"Dream," I shout.

"Jasper?"

"Dream."

"Jasper?"

Tenaya is sat on the side of her bed, nudging my shoulder with her elbow. Her skin is cold. She's wearing the white summer dress and holding two cups of tea.

"Morning," she says.

I paw at my eyes then smile up at her. I want to cry, but I don't.

"Morning."

I take the tea she passes to me and pull myself up into a sitting position.

"Mum's drunk," she says. "She told me that Dad has fucked off and that he's never coming back."

"Are you okay?"

"I've been waiting for him to go. If he goes, Mum won't have anyone to argue with."

"She could argue with you."

"I'll try to stay away."

"Do you think it'll get better?"

"I don't know.

"Okay."

23

It is important to pass these upcoming exams for several reasons:

— So that Mum's face does not become red and her voice does not get loud and she does not stop giving me money to buy beers and drugs.

— So that I can do the next year of sixth form and not have to worry about getting a job and participating in life for one more year.

— So that I can get into university and not have to worry about getting a job or participating in life for three more years.

— So that Georgia Treely will think I am a man who is going places and who will be a good, hardworking father to her children.

— So that Tenaya will not hit me.

I am in the bath thinking about these things. In my hands there is a Philosophy and Religion textbook. I am reading about how some people believe in God because they had visions of the Virgin Mary. There is a large picture of the Virgin Mary wearing a blue dress and looking quietly pleased. I am bored. The book says that humans can hallucinate due to extreme emotional distress. I wonder if I will hallucinate because of the emotional stress caused by Keith's constant murder-plotting. I hope I hallucinate Georgia Treely masturbating with a toothbrush.

I fold the textbook back on itself so that only the picture of the Virgin Mary is showing and I hold it in one hand. I move down into the water and hold the photograph directly over my head. I move it toward my face until the Virgin Mary's nose is almost touching my nose. The picture shivers in my hand as I masturbate. Afterward I sit back up and watch my semen floating sadly in islands on the bathwater.

Next the textbook covers the Trinity. There is no wank fodder on these pages so I just read for a while. The Trinity is a diagram of a triangle with *The Father*, *The Son*, and *The Holy Spirit* written on different corners with *THEY ARE ALL ONE!* written in the center. Haile Selassie was the name of an Ethiopian emperor and it means "the power of the Trinity." Rastafarians believe that he was Jesus. They stand on opposite sides of Copson Lane and shout his name at each other. Mum will not walk past them because she believes that if she inhales their secondhand marijuana smoke then she will become addicted to drugs and eventually die of a heroin overdose in a house where the walls are filled with dead mice.

I shampoo and condition my pubic hair, then my head hair, and then I step out of the bath. I pull a towel around my waist and tuck it into itself so that it will stay there without me holding it. Mum is stood outside the bathroom door with her hands on her hips.

"Jasper," she says, "you have been in the bath for over an hour."

"Mum," I say, "it is illegal to interrogate people who are not wearing any clothes."

"What were you doing?"

I wave the Philosophy and Religion textbook in her face.

"I was revising," I say. "I am going to make you extremely proud, Mum."

She makes a sound like "hmm," then pushes past me into the bathroom.

In my room I download and watch a Serbian film about a man who believes that his wife is a ghost. In one scene they have sex and afterward he says, "For a ghost, baby, you're pretty good," and then she hits him and leaves the room.

When all the blue in the sky has been soaked up by clouds, I sit at my desk and recommence work on my novel. I make notes about a man who builds a hut in a forest and uses it to rape girls in. When he has raped them he uses a butter knife to chop their bodies into small pieces, which he bakes into sausage rolls and feeds to his schizophrenic mother. I think it is important to write about things like this. It is important because things like this often happen, mainly in America. Usually it is men with mustaches that do things like this, for example Keith.

Possible novel titles:

And the Trees Said Nothing
Get in My Car and You Will Become Famous
Forced in Tree
She Woodknot
Sexual Bat-Tree

I stare at my hands for a while. I think about all the bad things people have ever done. I realize that I am going to have to phone the police and do an anonymous tip-off and tell them about Keith and what he has done. Margaret Clamwell's body was probably buried too deep for me to uncover using only my hands. When the police learn of the body's whereabouts they will dig up the entire garden, twice. I will have to do the tip-off just before I leave for the end-of-exams party at the cottage because if Mum finds out then she will not let me go.

Carrie Waterman is having a house party tomorrow. Tenaya already said she wouldn't go because she had to revise. I decide to phone Jonah and ask if he's going.

He answers after two rings.

"Sup?" he says.

"Not much, just bored. You going to that thing tomorrow?"

"Carrie's?"

"Yeah."

"No, Mum says I have to stay in."

"What? Why?"

"Not sure. Pope's on telly, I think."

"The pope? Why do you still care about him? Didn't he like rape kids or something?"

"No, that was Irish priests."

"Catholic ones?"

"Yeah."

"Mum says you are who you associate with."

"He's apologizing."

"Apologies never fixed anyone's torn asshole."

"Guess not."

"So you aren't coming?"

"Can't, man. Sorry."

"It's fine."

"Night."

"Yeah."

I hang up.

I stare at the exam timetable pinned to the corkboard above my desk. It does not look exciting.

I watch old episodes of *QI* on BBC iPlayer. I wish Stephen Fry weren't gay and my mum could marry him and he could teach me things like how you can hurt someone more when you're wearing boxing gloves than when you aren't. The only thing that Keith has taught me is constant vigilance.

As a way of avoiding revision, I fill out a long questionnaire on Facebook. This is called "procrastination."

1. *Your ex is on the side of the road, on fire, what do you do?*
   can we do that thing where you break up with someone but then have sex again once or maybe twice afterward please
2. *Your best friend tells you she's pregnant, what is your reaction?*
   you are going to be a very good mother. i believe in you.
3. *When was the last time you wanted to punch someone in their face?*
   this is gay
4. *Congratulations! You just had a son, what's his name?*
   martin Luther king
5. *Congratulations! You just had a daughter, what's her name?*
   simone olive buckettwat
6. *What are you craving right now?*
   an end to institutionalized racism
7. *What is your favorite sexual position?*
   the "penis in vagina" position

8. *Do you like pickles?*

   no

9. *What color is your crotch?*

   hazelnut brown

10. *What is in your pocket?*

    hummus

11. *Say you were given a pregnancy test right now, would you pass or fail?*

    chance would be a fine thing

12. *Have you ever blocked someone on Facebook before?*

    you shouldn't have done that

13. *Do you know anyone in jail/prison?*

    yes. no. sorry, I'm embarrassed. that was really really childish. i don't want to do this anymore

+

Because I am stressed about the possible repercussions of implicating Keith in the disappearance of the girl, I am suffering insomnia. It is 3:46 a.m. One of the things I do when I can't sleep is to research insomnia and sleep deprivation. Here are some facts about insomnia:

— There is little to no increase in mortality associated with insomnia. In fact, there seems to be an increase in life expectancy.

— Somniphobia is a fear of sleep.

— Thai Ngoc is a Vietnamese insomniac who claims to have gone without sleep for thirty-three years.
— Sleep deprivation has shown potential as a treatment for depression. Such treatment is called Wake Therapy.

I attempted Wake Therapy when I thought I had meningitis but I fell asleep.

It is 3:51 a.m. If I can't sleep by five, then I sit in the dew outside, drink cups of strong, sweet tea and watch the morning. I enjoy being outdoors during mornings and evenings because I find that the sky is much more creative in its use of color. For instance, gray may be substituted for fuchsia, saffron, salmon or other romantically named hues of red.

I go to www.girlsoncam.com, enter my nickname as "Ebonylonghorn" and click "enter room."

You: hi, babe
Candywife: hey, baby, how are you?
You: horny, babe. you?
Candywife: horny for you too, babe. wanna go private?

No.

You: can you show me some of your bod before we go private, babe?

She stretches out over her bed so that I can see her

mediocre middle-aged body. The skin around her thighs is bunched up and pockmarked and her stomach hangs down like a thick slab of chicken over her waistline. She is an average model for the MILF category.

You: mmmm
Candywife: ;)
Candywife: private now?

I decide that I am bored. I decide to use Wikipedia to unbalance her. I am going to inject confusion into her strange and distant life.

You: what will you do in private?
Candywife: anything you want, bb
You: will you brush your teeth?

Pause.

Candywife: sure, babe, in private
You: can you do it now, please? i don't want to wind up in a plaque show!
Candywife: in private, babe
You: once i paid for a girl to go private and then she wouldn't brush her teeth
Candywife: I'm not like that, babe
You: i don't know that, please
Candywife: fine, fine
Candywife: you had best go private

Candywife crawls grudgingly off her bed. She is wearing lilac underwear and a stained taupe bra. As she moves I can see that her pubic hair remains untamed, extending down the insides of her thighs and up the wrinkled crescent moon of the valley between her buttocks.

After two minutes she returns and bares her pixelated teeth at the webcam. Candywife thinks that she is a wolf in sheep's clothing. She thinks that I am prey.

You: babe, you are supposed to brush for three minutes

Candywife: what?

You: spend one minute on the lower jaw, one on the upper, and the remaining minute can be used to attack the plaque on the reverse side of the teeth, to brush the gums, or to brush the tongue

Pause.

I think about how her father will maybe hit her if she makes no money. I think about how his voice probably sounds like a monsoon of gravel and vodka. Because he does not know what else to do. I do not know what else to do. I am not being very sensitive today.

Candywife: go private

You: you haven't brushed your teeth properly

Candywife: i did what you said
You: i am only looking out for you
You: decay in a tooth can cause a cavity. if the decay continues, infection of the tissue within the pulpal chamber will occur, which will result in necrosis, and necrosis, if unabated, can affect the jawbone
You: it's true, I'm reading about it right now
You: on Wikipedia
You: so it's definitely definitely true
You: and if you have a wonky jaw, no one will go private with you

Pause.

Candywife: please go private

I watch my monitor in fascination as a single tear trips down her cheek. She tilts her head down. Candywife has bleached-blonde hair with faint copper roots. I wonder if she knows that the sound of crying can trigger "the milk ejection reflex" in the mothers of newborns. When I think about this I imagine Mum, just after having me, watching a film with Dad. In the film a baby cries because goblins have surrounded its crib and are dancing. Milk begins to dribble from Mum's nipples and permeate her T-shirt. This makes Dad want to do sex with her but then I start crying so they can't. Sorry, Dad.

You: knock knock

Candywife: what

You: knock knock

Candywife: Who's there?

You: disco

Candywife: disco who

You: disconnect

I log off.

It is 4:06 a.m. Fifty-four minutes until the point of no return.

It would be best to work on my novel in the shed. In the shed, I will be able to feel the rapist's motivations better.

I slowly toe my way into the garden, wearing only boxer shorts and a duvet. I am worried that Keith will wake up and kill me with a spade or other blunt garden tool then bury me under the apple tree with Margaret Clamwell and any of his other victims I have yet to find out about. Margaret Clamwell will be undergoing putrefaction at present. This is the second stage of decomposition, characterized by the abdomen turning green due to bacterial activity and a buildup of gases that force liquids and feces out of the body. I am not prepared for this to happen to me yet. If I see Keith, I will fight him. I will stab him in the eye with my Biro and I will click it repeatedly once I get it in. This is called "adding insult to injury." My e-mail to Abby Hall also falls into this bracket.

Sat under the duvet in the shed, using my phone as a torch, I chew the end of my pen until it resembles roadkill. I can't write. I try to remember and draw as many different Mr. Men as I can. I score four. I fall asleep.

24

During the exam period, Mum makes me write revision timetables every day and put them on the fridge. Most days I wake up at lunchtime, watch the ceiling from bed for a while, then go downstairs. I eat Weetabix and smoke and write a timetable to make Mum happy. Usually I am still very tired so I just write:

7:00 a.m. – wake up
Entire Day – revise
11:00 p.m. – sleep

Next I shift magnetic words around on the fridge to make positive-sounding sentences that will make Mum feel optimistic about the future of her only son.

me i am a happy love man tree and red
man love
happy tree man and me
am i a man

All of the exams are either in the early morning or midafternoon. For the afternoon exams I wake up at lunchtime and eat, then walk to school. For the morning exams I wake up at seven, then walk to school, then walk to Tenaya's for tea. Sometimes while I am at her house she tries to make me revise in front of her. She folds her face into a strange shape and tells me that she wants me to do well. One day Tenaya will be a very good mother.

At school my desk number is 86. This works out at being near the front. Oscar Chao sits next to me. Every time over the two-month period I see him sitting an exam, he wears the same socks. They are lilac with yellow thunderbolts on them. They are his lucky socks, I think. I don't know why. Maybe he lost his virginity while wearing them to a girl that has done catalogue modeling.

I do not have lucky socks. I have an overwhelming sense of impending failure.

+

My relaxed, stress-free exam routine is only punctured once, by a phone call that goes like this:

"Jasper?"

"Who is it?"

"Abby."

"Uh. Hi, Abby."

"My period is late by two weeks."

Pause.

"My period is late by two weeks, Jasper."

"THEN FUCKING HURRY IT UP."

Tears (not mine).

"I think I'm pregnant, Jasper."

"I'm sorry, I think you have the wrong number."

"Jasper, please."

"WHAT?"

"I think I'm pregnant, Jasper."

"THEN GET A FUCKING ABORTION, NOW."

I hang up.

I am insensitive and cruel.

I am scared.

There is no fucking way Abby Hall is going to ruin The Georgia Plan with her weird little baby.

Fuck. Fuck. Fuck.

25

3:29 p.m. I am sat in Julia's office, thinking of how I first came to see Julia. Trying not to think of babies or fatherhood. In my head, it is summer 2009. Memory is escape. Me and Tenaya are sat on a short brick wall down off the end of my road. We are rolling cigarettes. We are supposed to be revising for mock GCSEs.

On one side of the wall is the front garden of number 46 Chestnut Crescent. On the other side is a river of pavement that meets Ivythorne Road.

We are looking at the sun.

"Jasper?" Tenaya asks.

"Yeah."

"One day we will be old."

We look at the sun some more. It melts and forms lakes over the concrete, grass and brick.

"Yeah, I guess so. Unless we get murdered or we contract AIDS or we get run over by buses or we choose to end our lives because of unbearable emotional turmoil."

"But statistically, we will probably get old."

"Yeah," I say. "We will."

"That means being married and having children."

"Statistically."

"Yeah, but I don't want children."

"So?"

"Well, I will probably want children when I'm old, right?"

"I suppose."

She throws her cigarette into the garden and rests her head in a cradle made from her hands.

"Does that mean I will be a different person?"

"No."

"Yes, it does."

"No, it doesn't."

"But I will think differently."

"People are fickle."

"I don't want to be a different person."

"Why not?"

"I don't know."

I pinch her.

"There," I say, "now you are a—"

Mum comes strolling round the corner, speaking to someone angrily through her blue plastic hands-free thing. She doesn't see us straightaway because her eyes are sprawled across the new gypsy-laid driveway of number 32. Tenaya pulls me by the collar, off the wall and into the garden of number 46.

That was when I fell onto the cat.

It takes a remarkably long amount of time before either of us realizes what has happened. The cat is doing a sort of breathless screaming. It is really flat below me, as though we are in a scene from *Tom and Jerry*.

I have to stay lying on the cat until Mum has disappeared round the corner. During this time it has few muscles left intact with which to form a resistance. Then me and Tenaya stand up around the cat and look down over it, a pair of inexperienced and slightly queasy young gods.

"Fucking kill it," Tenaya says.

She always expects me to be the proactive one because I am a boy.

"I don't want to kill it, you kill it."

"You're the one that crushed it."

"You're the one that likes cats," I say, not entirely convinced of my defense.

"What?!"

I look down at the cat. Its eyes have been forced forward out of its tiny skull. It is convulsing in spasms like an epileptic. I wonder how aware it is.

"Fucking kill it!" Tenaya shouts.

Because of panic and an aggressive sense of conscience, I opt for a regretfully crude form of euthanasia. I kick the cat's head against the wall—hard. This results in the wide blooming of a corduroy firework composed of brain and blood. My right foot in particular is heavily redecorated.

Because Time has been around for a long time, it often gets bored. In order to briefly relieve its boredom, Time enjoys constructing massively unlikely series of events. If these events are of the romantic kind, they are called Fate; and if they are of the negative kind, we call them Unfortunate Coincidence.

An Unfortunate Coincidence occurs next, because the bald, liver-spotted man from number 46 wanders out of his house immediately after I have dealt his cat the deathblow with my boot. There are still brains on it.

We panic.

We run, even though it is no use because he knows my mum. I think we wanted to avoid the confrontation. There was still confrontation with my mum, but not with Keith. Keith tends to avoid confrontation. If the potential for debate ever arises, he says, "Let's agree to disagree." I wonder how he will argue his case in court. Probably using a shotgun that fires crocodile tears and a tie that screams "Good Christian man."

In the end Mum said, "You are a heartless psycho," and I said, "It was an accident," and Keith said, "Let's agree to disagree," and then I got Julia. Which is where I am now.

Julia has a brighter face today. Maybe someone has

decided that they love her. Maybe she has a boyfriend who runs marathons and calls her Jillybean. Maybe they sit together in the evenings drinking cheap wine and watching films with Hugh Grant in them.

I think about trying to get advice about Abby Hall's baby out of Julia. Julia will probably try to convince me to become a Father. I will meet Abby's ugly child every weekend in a motorway McDonald's because I will be too embarrassed to meet it at a McDonald's in town. The child will try to get me to give it money. I will tell it to please leave me alone.

The light in Julia's room today is like a morning sea seen by sad sailors. That is a bad metaphor that means there is light but it does not feel warm. It is a gray-white that falls in stretched shapes across the carpet. Julia is clicking her pen and looking at me expectantly. She has just asked about Tabitha Mowai.

"It made me feel sad," I say.

I remember that Julia thinks I am racist. Sometimes, if you tell enough lies, they gang together and do this type of bullying where one crouches down behind you and the other one pushes you over them. This is what my lies are doing now.

"It did?" Julia asks.

"Yes," I say. "I am not really a racist. Sorry."

Julia smiles. "I know."

"What?"

"I know that you are not a racist, Jasper. You are a good kid. You just let your imagination carry you away a little sometimes." That is called a cliché.

I stare openmouthed at Julia for a while. I am wondering whether she has performed some sort of clever psychological trick on me by pretending to be moronic during our time together. Maybe she is an extremely clever female who could provide me with a foolproof arsenal of seduction techniques.

"Um," I say.

"What counts," Julia explains, "is that you are growing out of it. It seemed likely that you would and you are. Your mum just wanted you to come here so that we could be sure."

"But I am definitely gay," I say. "And Sebastian is definitely real."

Julia smiles again.

She stands up and walks around the desk and bends down to embrace me in a small hug. Her hair rubs against my face. It smells of mango.

"I think this will be the last time we need to see each other," Julia says.

And it is.

PART 3

Rains and Cattle

26

12:52 a.m. I'm in bed. Radio 4 is on. I am listening to the shipping forecast. The shipping forecast is an extremely comfortable duvet. If they had played the shipping forecast during the Somme then everyone would have dropped their guns and crawled into their sleeping bags and talked about the makeup of stars until morning.

Viking North Utshire South Utshire Southeast

Before the shipping forecast they play "Sailing By"; afterward they play the national anthem. Sometimes, when I am drunk, I like to sit up in bed and sing along with the national anthem and try to imagine what it would be like to genuinely believe that being born in a certain place at a certain time is something to be proud of. Doing sex with a girl for over seven minutes is something to be proud of. Being British is not.

Four or five, increasing six or seven, veering south four or five later

British people watch charity pleas for Ethiopian AIDS orphans on television and tell each other it makes them feel sad. They call it a shame that some people starve to death. Sometimes they pick up the phone and arrange for three pounds to leave their bank accounts every month.

Occasional rain, good

Nobody asks for Ethiopian AIDS orphans to all be allowed into Britain, though. The country is ours. And the televisions. And the shoes. And the roast dinners. I don't think we would act that way if we were all Ethiopians. I don't think we would say, "Nobody is allowed into this country. It is ours. And the dirty water. And the bloated bellies. And the AIDS."

With fog patches, becoming moderate or poor

I look at the ceiling. My head is filled with sailors on a huge oil tanker, huddled around their radio, swigging Captain Morgan. They are alone in the middle of a black sea. Clouds of fog drift across the reflection of a dandelion moon. Later, in their hammocks, they talk about missing their wives and children. They will sway in their sleep with the six or seven wind.

I am sleepy. I am trying only to think about sailors and not about Abby Hall's fetus. I have decided not to tell anyone about the baby. I have decided not to think about the baby. I have decided that, if necessary, I will use blackmail to get her to abort it.

Get an abortion, Abby, or else I will poison your dog.

Go to sleep. Do not think about Abby Hall's baby. If you do not think about it then it will go away. Abby Hall is a slut. The baby is not yours. What baby? Exactly.

My phone vibrates. Tenaya. *Jasper, I'm drunk and I'm alone and I want to speak to you.* I think about Tenaya standing in the kitchen with tea steam rising from between her hands and a pile of paracetamol on the table. I text back, *bridge, 15 mins.* I will sacrifice my sleep for her arms.

Mum and Keith went to sleep at ten. They will be lost in the dull suburban forests of their dreams by now. I pull on jeans and a gray hoodie. I take some money from the Doctor Who money box by my bed, push it into my pocket and toe down the stairs like a ninja. The door is on my side. It closes very quietly behind me.

The night outside is cold and distant. It is a huge blanket. It covers me, and Tenaya, and Abby Hall, her fetus, and the sailors in their hammocks, and their missing wives, and the ocean they have started to hate. I power walk along our street, past the rows of sycamores planted into holes in the pavement and hidden by the night. Silhouettes do sex in window frames.

At the Happy Shopper I flatten my hair, breathe in and step inside. A woman with sad eyes is reading a pink paperback at the counter. I stride up to the till. Confidence is the key to success.

"Two bottles of your cheapest white wine," I say.

She looks me up and down. She takes two bottles off the shelf behind her and places them on the counter.

"You got ID?" she says.

"ID?" I shout. "ID?" Getting louder. "I'm twenty-five years old, for fuck's sake. I've got a fucking five-year-old child and everything." I feel sick; in five years' time, this might be true. I feel guilty also, but I need to save Tenaya.

She sighs. "Okay," she says, taking my money. "You aren't something to do with the police?"

"I'm absolutely not," I say, taking a wine bottle in each hand. "But I am very sorry for shouting."

I run with the bottles up to the motorway bridge. Tenaya is already sat at the highest point, cross-legged, facing away from town. I drop down beside her and pass her a bottle. She breathes an arm of smoke out into the night.

"Thanks, Jasper," she says.

I light a cigarette.

"It's okay. Are you fine?"

"I don't know."

"It can't last forever."

"I know."

I look down below us at the strips of headlights and taillights, rivers red and white. The streetlight overhead covers our legs with orange glow. We are out of the currents. I feel as though I am stood shoulder to shoulder with Tenaya at the edge of the world, looking down at everything.

"So," I say, "what did you want to speak about?"

"I didn't want to speak *about* anything."

"You said you wanted to talk to me."

Tenaya rests her head on my shoulder. I swig from the wine. I do not understand her. I understand that she is upset and that I want to help. I am not equipped with the tools necessary to fix emotional imbalance.

"You don't have to say anything," she says. "We can just sit."

I will not tell Tenaya about the thing in Abby Hall's womb. I do not want to burden her with my baby. My baby. Baby. I am definitely not going to be a Dad.

Get an abortion, Abby, or else I will tell *Hello!* magazine that you are Michael Jackson's secret daughter.

A man pulls onto the side of the road. He steps out of his car. He is pressing a mobile phone against his ear. He holds it there, stuck between his shoulder and cheek, then puts a cigarette into his mouth and lights it. Tenaya quietly burps. The man paces and makes frantic hand gestures while talking into the phone. He is Tony Blair. His hands are weapons.

"He's talking to his wife," Tenaya says. "He's telling her that he's had enough and he's not coming back."

"He's talking to his boss," I say. "He's told him he's a bastard and that he can go and fuck himself."

"He's answering a newspaper advert for casual homosexual sex."

"He's telling his daughter he wants to fuck her."

"Nice, Jasper."

"Sorry."

We both stand up and lean over the railings. The man is holding his phone in an outstretched hand. He is staring at it as though it is a dismembered anus.

"Looks like he's been told someone's dead or something," Tenaya says.

"Yeah."

"Seems sad."

"If you died, I would set something big on fire. The school, or the cathedral."

"Thanks, Jasper."

I sit back down. Tenaya follows. We light two more cigarettes.

"I am going to seduce Georgia Treely in Devon," I say.

"With what?"

"Not with Rohypnol."

"How nice."

"With my roguish good looks and wit."

Tenaya laughs.

"What?" I say.

"Nothing."

Small white hills jump out of Tenaya's arms. She is cold. The wind here is waking up. It is a nocturnal sprinter.

"Are you okay?"

"Better, thanks."

We finish our wine bottles, smash them and walk back into the suburb.

27

My last exam is Psychology Paper 2, which started at 9:15 a.m. It is now 10:30 a.m. I have already finished and am looking around the room at everyone else. Georgia Treely finished ten minutes ago but she has been going over her paper again and again. I hope she does very well. She will definitely do very well. Eventually she will own a converted barn in an area of the Midlands where teenage girls put posters of David Cameron on their walls. Jonah stopped writing half an hour ago and he is drawing penises with faces on the back of his paper.

Finally we are told to put down our pens and leave. Everyone cheers except for Oscar Chao, who still has a Chinese exam to do in the afternoon. The exam invigilator turns purple and shouts that we are still under exam conditions and not to make any noise until we have left the exam venue. Everyone cheers again and rushes to leave.

Tenaya is stood outside the school gates, waiting for me. She is holding two cigarettes. One for me, one for her. Her last exam was History, which was two days ago.

"How was it?" she says. We begin walking toward the Yellow Pony. It is a pub frequented mainly by old men but we go there because they do not ask for ID.

"It was okay," I tell her. "It seemed fine."

"You best have passed, Jasper."

"I know."

"Because if you haven't, I am going to rip your dick off."

I grin. "Okay."

She punches my arm.

I wonder how she will punish me for getting Abby Hall pregnant.

Not pregnant.

Definitely not pregnant.

Jonah is already sat in the Yellow Pony, behind a beer and a Murakami novel. I do not understand much about Jonah but I understand why he reads Murakami. Murakami makes me feel safe and positive. I wish Murakami was my stepdad. Murakami would never murder my mum.

"Morning," Jonah says. Tenaya goes over to the bar to get our drinks. "Good exam?"

"Great," I say. "What time are we going tomorrow?"

I am imagining waking up in the morning and going

downstairs to find Haruki Murakami drinking coffee and reading *The Guardian* at our kitchen table.

"Not sure. Come round, like, four, I guess."

So, Dad, what have you been working on lately?

"Who else are you taking? Tenaya is going with Ping and Ana because she has to stay at home later for some family thing."

Murakami wouldn't call me patronizing names.

"Oh, shit, yeah. Forgot to tell you. I got us two girls. We're taking them."

"What? Who?"

"Susan Pilkington and Jenna Slater," he says.

I recognize the names. They are girls from the year below. I imagine their faces. Pretty good.

"They're quite fit," I say.

"Yeah," he says. "They are."

Tenaya comes back over and puts down a Newcastle for me and Carling for her. She nods toward the book on the table.

"Is that the one where he fucks his sister, then his mum?" she asks.

"But he only fucks his sister in a dream," I say.

"Okay," Jonah says. "Don't ruin it."

Murakami would definitely make a very good replacement stepdad.

28

I wake up at twelve and go downstairs. Mum and Keith are both at work. I pull all of the revision timetables off the fridge and throw them into the bin. Standing in boxer shorts with the sun glancing off my cheeks, I feel positive and okay. The party tonight will be good. Georgia Treely will be there. Prepare to be seduced, Georgia Treely.

First, though, there is something I have to do.

Sat on the white leather sofa in our living room, I take out my phone. I type in 1-4-1 to hide my number, and then put in the number for the police station. A woman answers.

"West Midlands Police, how can I help?" she says.

"Hello," I say, "I would like to do an anonymous tip-off, please."

"Okay, of what."

The way the woman says "okay" stretches out the *o* until it is the shape of a rugby ball.

"Of a murder."

"A murder?"

"Yes," I say. "I know who murdered that girl who died last week and the same man also murdered a woman called Margaret Clamwell and he plans to murder again."

"Okay," the woman says. She stretches the *o* out again. "And what evidence do you have for this?"

"Lots of evidence," I assure her. Then I very quickly tell her my address and hang up.

I go upstairs.

I stand in front of the bathroom mirror, preparing to prepare myself for the seduction of Georgia Treely. The Georgia Plan. Should I put gel in my hair? Is gel gay?

People who wear gel in their hair:

Robert Pattinson in *Twilight*
Hugh Grant in *Bridget Jones's Diary*
Neo in *The Matrix*

Yes, I should definitely wear gel.

I sculpt my hair into polished waves then move it close to the mirror.

"What a great face," I say.

I move closer to the mirror.

"What a great face," I say again, this time louder.

I remain unconvinced.

I run my hands along my jawbones. They feel prickly. Shaving routine: once every two weeks. Should I remove the prickles early? I decide to leave them. They will make me look mature. Georgia Treely will be tricked into thinking that I am a real human man. Really all I am is cunning.

There is a spot on my left eyebrow. It is perfectly circular and yellow. It nestles amongst the hairs like a small child hiding in woods. I squeeze the pus from it and carry the trophy through into my room on the tip of my right index finger. I wipe it on the small, star-shaped mirror in my bedroom. Where possible, I have been leaving all such trophies on display across this mirror since the age of fifteen. They fly in long smears, smudged at odd angles like dull fireworks reflected in a lake of metal. It is a piece of contemporary art. Soon, Charles Saatchi will offer to buy this mirror from me. He will make me an offer I can't refuse.

+

When I go round to Jonah's at four, he is still sleeping. The door is open so I go inside. Upstairs I pull off his duvet and slap his ass and shout, "Get up, you prick," and he shouts back, "Fuck off, Jasper," but eventually he gets up. We both sit on the end of his bed, him picking the moondust out of his eyes and complaining.

With his eyes cleared Jonah turns on his laptop and

plays Leftöver Crack. He dresses quickly then rolls a joint. We smoke it sat in his conservatory with cups of tea. It takes him a long time to properly wake up. It is very bright and warm in the conservatory. The sky is yellow and starting to fall.

"Where are we picking them up?" I ask.

"Outside the Argos in town, at half past."

"We should leave."

"Yeah," Jonah says. He crushes the joint out in an ashtray.

"Jonah?"

"Yeah."

"What's up?"

"What do you mean?"

He taps at his phone. I imagine he is just scrolling through contacts so that he doesn't have to look at me.

"Just you seem . . . ," I say. I pause. "I don't know, off. You haven't said anything disgusting yet."

"It's nothing," he says. "We can talk later. Let's go pick up the gash."

I laugh. "Okay."

Susan Pilkington and Jenna Slater are stood waiting for us outside Argos. Susan has blonde hair and large, round breasts. She is wearing a floral skirt and white leggings. Jenna has very short, dark hair and smaller, more friendly-looking breasts. She is wearing tight jeans and an olive parka. They are both smiling and fidgeting and generally looking like nice, well-rounded human females.

Jonah grins and leans over to push open the front

passenger door. Susan Pilkington climbs in beside him. This means that he has allocated Jenna Slater to me. This is okay because big breasts scare me anyway.

Jenna Slater climbs in next to me.

"Hello," she says, smiling brightly. She doesn't know that I'm going to be a Dad.

"Hello," I say.

I try my best to smile. It probably looks retarded. I wonder if this is going to be like the last time I picked up girls with Jonah. No. It can't be like that. These girls are young and sexually attractive and nice.

"How are you?" she asks.

I can hear Jonah fluently conversing with Susan in the front. He is good at understanding what girls want to hear. I used to be good at that but I think I have forgotten how to do it.

Time to try my best. Mum says that as long as I try my best, no one can ask any more of me.

"Uh," I say, "I'm okay. I'm really really okay." I look around the car. Through the window I can see a toddler chewing the hem of her mother's skirt. "How are you?"

She grins again. Wider. "I'm really great," she says. "The party will be good."

"The party will be good," I repeat dumbly. I am stupid. I should probably pretend to be asleep throughout this entire journey.

The drive down to Devon takes an hour and a half. Jonah makes Susan hold a map that he printed off using

Google Maps and read directions. Whenever she speaks, she doesn't seem very sure. Jonah said that he wasn't going to drink and drive but he quickly gets frustrated and insists I pass him forward a beer, which I do, because I am a good friend.

Talking with Jenna becomes easier and easier after beers and a few joints. Jenna enjoys talking so I do not have to do much. Jonah's driving becomes worse and worse, and after he almost collides with a caravan that has a LOVE LIFE bumper sticker on it, Susan makes him pull over at a motorway service station and drink a coffee. Jenna does not stop talking the whole time. I'm not bothered, really. Mostly I can't really make out the words and it is quite relaxing listening to her. It is like listening to Radio 4.

Some of the things Jenna talks about:

— How Jesus is actually a pretty great guy and even though everyone is fucking up everything he still loves them because that's just the way he is.
— How playing in the National Youth Jazz Orchestra is really fun because you get to meet lots of exciting new people who tell you exciting stories that you can then relate to Jasper Wolf because he is trapped in a car with you and can't run away.
— How it would be just lovely to move to Paris in the future because Paris is romantic.
— How all of the countries in the world should stop buying guns and start buying disco balls.

— How Ludovico Einaudi is, like, a genius.

— How *Amélie* is, like, the best film ever.

— How blonde hair might look better but it might also look less sophisticated but I could maybe try it I suppose just with, like, a home-dye kit from like Boots or something. I don't know. What do you think, Jasper?

I stare at her a while. "Oh," I say. "Yeah. Yeah, you look great."

Back in the car I down a can of beer and smoke a cigarette with my head leaning out of the window. I look forward down the motorway at lanes full of impatient cars and up at the bonfire sky with its sun slowly sliding into the hills. Jenna falls asleep on my shoulder. I fall asleep with my cheek against the glass.

29

Because we are sleeping, me and Jenna miss Jonah and Susan's frantic arguments over *Where the fuck ever are we? This doesn't look like Devon* and when we wake up the car is already parked in a small muddy clearing on the edge of a wide poppy field. Jonah is stood smoking in the last of the sun and Susan is beside him. They have made up. They have put the past behind them.

We have had to park away from the house because Amanda thinks that if people park near the house they will ruin the grass and Amanda's parents will be angry. People will probably park near the house anyway.

I nudge Jenna awake and she half opens her eyes and smiles. She shifts up and kisses me on the cheek. I try to smile at her again. I am pleased that she hasn't started talking. Once we start kissing it will be okay because I can use my mouth as a weapon to silence her.

Jonah says that we need to walk across the field and into the wood, and in the wood we will find a waterfall with a small lake below it, which is where Polly will meet us. Polly will lead us up to the cottage. I ask why it's Polly Who's taking us but Jonah shrugs.

Polly is a Polish boy with an effeminate face. His real name is Krasicki or something. It is probably slightly racist to call him Polly but he doesn't seem to mind.

We take full rucksacks out of the car boot and start moving through the low light of the field. Susan removes her shirt, and me and Jonah remove ours, leaving the sun to run down our shoulders, following the tracks of our spines and forming small pools of light between the poppy stems. Jonah carries the heavy pack with the ket stove and cans of beer in; I carry the rucksack containing drugs and hummus.

Me and Jenna quickly fall behind because she routinely pauses to swivel her neck and stare openmouthed at our surroundings.

"It's so beautiful out here," she says.

"Yeah," I say. "All green and lovely and things."

Definitely convincing.

"But people just don't seem to care about it anymore. They are letting nature be destroyed."

"Yep," I agree. I light a cigarette. "All this lovely grass

and stuff being replaced by people in houses with people in them. Just awful."

"People won't even give to charity anymore."

"Everyone should give to charity," I say.

I think charity is like putting a plaster on a man with no skin.

"I mean people just need to come out here and take in the beauty of nature, then they'll understand."

I loudly inhale through my nose and shut my eyes.

"So beautiful," I say.

Christ, what am I doing. I am going to need drugs.

Jonah stops and turns to face us.

"Let's stop here," he says. "I'm tired and I want a joint."

He and Susan sit down where they are. Me and Jenna walk to where they are and drop ourselves, too, crushing poppies beneath our buttocks.

We sit in a square. Jonah fumbles with King Rizla on top of his rucksack. The light is evaporating. The sky is honey and the air is thick and fat with pollen.

"Isn't it so beautiful out here?" Susan says to Jenna.

"It's amazing," Jenna says.

Jonah gives me a distressed look and I try not to laugh. There will be time for laughing after I have put my penis inside Jenna's vagina. I imagine her pubic hair is untamed, like the field of poppies we are sat in. Maybe I will get her pregnant, too. Stop getting people pregnant, Jasper. You are not Dad material.

Get an abortion, Abby, or else I will put a horse head on my head and come into your room late at night.

I will stirrup her life and teach her to stop saddling innocent people with ugly babies.

I have astounding wit.

I do not have Georgia Treely.

I wonder if the police have arrested Keith yet. I wonder if they have sent electric shocks through his genitals in order to obtain a confession. I wonder if Mum is relieved because she has realized what a lucky escape she has had. I am a very good son for stopping her murder. She will probably buy me a Mini Cooper.

We all doze for a while as the joint is passed around. Jonah lies on his back with his head rested up on his rucksack. Susan rests her head in his lap and ties knots in her yellow hair. Jenna smiles at me and I try to smile back but I can't think of anything to say. She looks expectant.

I pick a poppy and hold it in my hand.

"Heroin is made from poppies," I say. "Sherlock Holmes smoked opium."

"Oh," Jenna says.

I think about how it is illegal to sell drugs made from plants that grow everywhere but it is not illegal to manufacture a drug in a laboratory and sell it on the Internet. At least people know what the long-term health effects of heroin are, and how to deal with them. You know that if you start taking heroin then your hair will eventually turn to dreadlocks and you will eventually die. People barely even know what designer drugs are. When our generation grows up, we might all get Parkinson's or something.

Jonah sits up and rummages in his rucksack. He pulls out a four-pack of cheap Polish beers and throws them into the center of our square.

"You are all drinking," he says. "I'm tired of carrying all this shit around."

We all open beers and sit back sipping them. I can just make out the lip of the sun up over the edge of the distance. A faint vellum moon is already hung in the sky, in between suggestions of small stars.

"The moon," Jenna says happily.

"Oh, wow," I say. "The moon."

Jonah laughs and his mouthful of beer jumps forward in a shower. It freckles Susan's skin but she says nothing.

Jenna lies back and a wide band of skin is exposed across her stomach from where her T-shirt has pulled up. I light a Richmond and leave it burning in the corner of my mouth while I pluck the petals off a poppy and lie them flat over Jenna's belly button. This is called "flirting." Flirting is a door with sex behind it. Sex is a door with babies behind it. Fucking doors. People should keep them locked.

"We should probably move. Polly will be waiting," Jonah says.

Jenna stands up and the petals tumble off of her stomach and we all get up and shoulder our rucksacks.

There are only a few meters up to where the field meets the wood. Once we pass between the first trees the light is reduced to pale colors that have slipped between high branches. Jonah says that we need to keep following the path until we reach the pool.

It is half an hour before we find the waterfall and its adjoining pool in the sticky gloom of the wood. Polly is perched on a boulder, cigarette between his lips, waiting. I throw down my rucksack. Jonah walks over and talks briefly with Polly. Polly rarely smiles. He walks back over to us.

"Let's swim," he says, a grin across his face.

We all stand and watch the waterfall. It is high and slim, the width of a Labrador laid on its side, falling down and converging with a long pool hemmed at random intervals by mossy rocks. As it falls the water looks a jumbled, fuzzy white, but settled in the pool it takes on a sad hue of green.

"Really?" Susan says.

"Yes, really. Why not?"

"Doesn't it look a bit green?" Jenna says.

"No," Jonah explains. "You need to think of it more as an emerald."

In order to turn the sad green into emerald, we all have lines of mephedrone racked up on Susan's compact mirror.

Jenna is hesitant but I explain that it is a legal drug and you can buy it off the Internet. This convinces her. Easy.

It does not take long for the water to start appearing more attractive. The unwell green transforms into a green the hue of freshly mown summer grass. I look Jenna over. She has changed from being a passable target into a Grecian bronze. I am captivated by the way her slight body sinks effortlessly into soft arched hips, down into sculpted thighs and salmon shins, right to her perfect hand-sized feet and faint peach toenails.

Next, the smiles come. One by one they spear our cheeks. We make a Mexican wave of wonky grins. We all undress while our limbs happily jerk and our mouths motor.

"I love all of you," Jonah says.

"People love war and money," I say.

"People should love each other. I love you."

Jenna turns and hugs me hard. I push my tongue inside her mouth and move it about.

"War and money can suck my dick."

"Let's all get married."

"Confetti!"

I feel the tickle of earth on my head. Jenna is throwing handfuls of it into the air.

"I love Polly, too."

"I love Pollyolly, too."

"We should tell him!"

"Marry him!"

More earth on my head, down my neck.

"Swim, he should swim with us."

"Or we should swim with him."

Everything blurs into a smudge of sound and color. I am a supernova explosion of goodwill.

We form a circle around Polly, who is still perched on his boulder, smoking. We are loving lions surrounding an injured gazelle. He looks resigned and faintly amused. Maybe it is mild fear, I can't tell. Everything looks wonderful.

"Polly, you are excellent," Susan says.

"Please swim."

"Swim."

"With us."

"Really sorry about everything."

"You are a super human."

"Superhuman."

"Uh, thanks," Polly says, shifting on his rock.

"I will have sex with you, I want to."

I see a hand reach out for Polly's crotch. We all swoop to enclose him in a fierce five-way bear hug that causes him to make an odd noise and then run off into the trees. We howl with laughter and throw ourselves into the emerald pool of cool water.

The water feels like winning a large cash prize. It seeps beneath our skins and makes us candles. Everything is bright and good.

"We are not the Internet Generation!"

"Fuck that."

"Fuck them!"

"Fuck televisions!"

"And Twitter."

"And Formspring."

"What's Formspring?"

"Never mind."

"I love you, Jonah."

"I love you, Jasper."

"I love you, Jenna."

"I love you, Susan."

The water is shallow enough for us to keep on our feet but we kick in somersaults through it. Walls of water grow up and fall away, turning through my hair and filling my mouth. Our tongues stain green. We laugh and laugh.

I stand pressed against Jenna. Her eyes climb inside mine. Her breasts held against my chest make me feel aware that they are the only parts of her body that will not fit into mine. I wish I had large dents in my chest for her breasts to press into so that we could be closer.

We touch noses.

"Eskimos," she whispers.

I scream.

She laughs.

We fall backward through the water, me on top, until she is lying on the pool bed squirming. When we break back through the surface our cheeks swell with still more laughter. Jenna looks beautiful. Her hair is flat and dark from the dirty water. It looks like melted chocolate.

Jonah and Susan are fitting their bodies together on the other side of the pool. She is making grunting sounds like a dying horse and his eyes are so wide it looks as though he has just seen his dead grandfather dressed as a woman giving the Queen a lap dance in the trees.

I place a hand on either side of Jenna's waist and let my pelvis advance through the water like Jaws. She tucks her face into the crook of my neck and then slides it up to my earlobe, where she bites. Blood. I scream and pull away.

"Sorry," she says. "I can't."

I paddle my way back to our landscape of discarded clothes and pull my boxer shorts back on. This is how Ping must feel. Crouched on Polly's boulder, I light the joint that Jonah has forgotten. I watch them have sex. The mephedrone is still painting my insides pink so I see it as beautiful. It makes me think how what people want most is to penetrate each other. Not just being around other humans, but being inside other humans. Submitting to other humans. Giving yourself up, naked and honest, to another human. Letting your mouth speak animal sounds in that other human's face. Listening to that other human speak sounds back at you.

Five minutes later Polly emerges from the trees and stands beside me, a cigarette limp in his lips. He runs a hand of fingers through his hair.

"It done near?" he says.

"Yeah, almost."

"Sovee?"

"Yeah."

"Yeah?"

"Yeah."

I know it is wearing off because his accent is starting to piss me off.

Polly flicks his cigarette butt into the pool and crosses his arms.

"Now we go," he says, loud but not shouting.

Jenna has been splashing herself, and Jonah and Susan are just cuddling now, so they all just giggle the last of the drugs up then climb out. While they re-dress and fumble with cigarettes, I try to quiz the Pole about who is at the party.

"So what girls are up there, then?" I ask, nodding into the trees.

"Sovee?"

"Girls?"

He points at Jenna's bare ass, the color of cooked chicken.

"Yeah."

"Hmmm." He looks around as though for answers. "Pakpak. Bac . . . bac . . . buc."

"What?"

"Buc . . . bacrrrr . . ."

I give up and walk over to steal a cigarette from Jonah. Mine have run out. I am hopeful of lots of females; it doesn't matter about Jenna. She wasn't that pretty, anyhow. She was strange and happy and dull.

"Comecome," Krasicki orders, setting off at a march into the wood. And we follow.

30

The cottage owned by Amanda Forthwart's parents is called Chinkapin Farm. It is large and squat and painted a color somewhere between pink and orange. The front is covered with trellises of ivy.

People are stood in circles smoking and drinking from cans of beer. The doors and windows of the house are wide open. I do not recognize many people. I cannot see Georgia Treely.

Inside, the carpets have already been marbled with mud and splashes of beer and cigarette butts. There are people on the sofas and cross-legged on the floor.

"Let's go upstairs," I say to Jonah. I pull him away from Susan and Jenna. If I cannot have sex with her then I do not want to be near her.

Upstairs, we find a guest bedroom with floral wallpaper.

The only person in it is a blonde girl passed out on the bed. We sit on the carpet and start up the small gas stove for cooking ket on.

Once the liquid is powder, we rack up lines on a Danielle Steel paperback that was on a shelf in the room. We take two up each nostril then lie back. The drips run like slug wakes down my throat.

"Jasper?" Jonah says.

"Yeah."

"Earlier, I was feeling funny because I was thinking."

"Yeah."

I can hear his voice but I don't really understand the words. I light a cigarette and look at the lines through my hands.

"I was just thinking how next year is our last year, right? And after that, we leave this town. And, I mean, I fucking hate this place but we've been here for, like, forever."

"Jonah?"

He pushes his hands against his eyes.

"Yeah."

"Are you scared?"

"No," he says, looking at the girl on the bed. "Fuck off."

"Yes, you are," I assure him. Everyone is scared.

"Don't be a queer."

"I'm scared," I say. I am being honest.

"You are?"

"Yeah." I light a cigarette. "Fuck the army, let's move to France. We can steal food and fuck girls from villages.

Or we can go to Canada and find a log cabin by a lake and fill it with wine and sluts."

"Jasper," he says, "I'm going to join the army. Now is for fucking about, later is for doing something. You can't fuck around forever."

"Why not?"

"Because if you try, you'll end up like Tenaya's parents."

I look at my hands. All the lines swim.

"Okay," I say.

"You want another line?"

"Sure."

"Then we should go back down."

"Okay. I am going to seduce Georgia Treely."

Jonah laughs.

After more lines, we do not go downstairs. We lie on our backs and stare at the ceiling. The plaster has been scraped into small waves. A modest chandelier hangs over our heads, kicking at the last of the light running in through a single window.

The blonde girl wakes up and ruffles her hair and flops off the bed. She stares at us with glassy, faraway eyes with nothing in them.

"You want a line?" Jonah says.

She nods.

I wonder who she is. I wonder if she ever lies in bed slapping her own face just to make sure she still can. I wonder what she sees in her head when she tries to think of what comes next.

I make a line up for her and she snorts it. She passes out again, this time over Jonah's lap. He pushes her off his trousers and onto the floor.

"Let's go back down," Jonah says.

Ping, Tenaya and Ana have arrived. Ping is sat by the television with Tenaya, Ana and six or seven other kids sat around him. He is holding a black metal cream-charger and cracking silver bullet-shaped canisters into brightly colored glitter balloons.

NOS balloons are religious experiences. They pull you right out of your place on Earth and put you right into nowhere. You stop having hands or feet or a head. Everything echoes. Everything echoes. Everything happens extremely slowly and jerkily, as though you're watching a video on YouTube using a dial-up connection. They only last half a minute or something.

You can buy a NOS charger and whippits off the Internet for not very much. It is called "hippie crack" sometimes.

I sit myself next to Tenaya. Her eyes are wet again. Maybe someone else has died. Maybe someone else has run off the edge of the planet. Tenaya is a very emotional human being. All human beings are very emotional. I am very emotional but I do not show it because if I do then people will think I am weak and they will mug me, emotionally.

"Hi," Tenaya says.

"What's wrong?" I ask.

"I haven't had NOS in a long time."

"What's wrong?" I repeat.

Tenaya points over her shoulder. Through the open door I can see Tom smoking outside next to a girl in a purple dress. They are holding hands. The girl is not wearing any shoes.

"That's my dress," Tenaya says.

"Prick," I say.

"Yeah."

I put my hand in Tenaya's hair and ruffle it affectionately. I am making her feel better.

"Get off, Jasper."

"Okay."

Ping passes us both balloons. Someone plays the song "Grow Up and Blow Away" by Metric. Music is a very important part of NOS. It gives you a ledge to watch things from. The song plays loud.

If this is the life
Why does it feel so good to die today?
Blue to gray
Grow up and blow away . . .

Ping counts up to three. On three, we all blow out then put the balloon necks into our mouths and begin inhaling and exhaling the pleasant-tasting gas. I can see Tenaya to my left. Her eyes are shut. Soon I can't see anything.

Everything I see and hear is reduced to a series of blurred circles, rotating over and over. The song slows into heavy ambience. Other sounds sway and replicate and jump apart.

The words of the song slow until they are still and sat in the air in front of me. *Grow Up and Blow Away.* I'm sat in the o of *Grow*. I'm swinging my legs. I climb through all the words in the chorus.

Tenaya's laughing but her eyes are still red. Things are focusing. There is laughter everywhere. Everyone has jumped up and is hugging and cheering like we have just fought a war and won.

31

Feeling fine. 1:30 a.m. I am stood in the kitchen talking to a girl who believes in angels. She tells me that my aura is blue. I tell her that she doesn't appear to have one. Ping appears. He grabs my arm and tells me to come with him into the cupboard under the stairs. He tells me I will need a beer.

The cupboard smells of damp. It is totally dark because Ping shut the door. I hold down buttons on my phone in order to extract light from it.

"Are you going to try and kiss me?" I say.

"Fuck off."

"What then?"

"It's about Abby Hall," Ping says. He sips from his beer. "About her baby."

I spit out the beer in my mouth like a bad actor.

"How the fuck do you know about that?"

"Abby told Ana."

"What the fuck did she tell Ana for?"

"Girl's don't seem to like Ana. She has to take all the friends she can get. Anyway, do you want the news or what?"

Something small dies in my stomach. "I don't know."

"You do."

I down the beer. "Okay."

"It's Ben McKay's."

I scream with laughter. Confetti. This is brilliant. This is the best possible way things could ever have turned out. I compose myself.

"What? When?"

"At Carrie Waterman's."

"But Abby's grounded," I say. "How did she go?"

"Right," Ping says. "But Ben McKay told her that he loved her so she sneaked out to see him."

I laugh loudly, again.

"Why did he say that?"

"He heard she was easy."

"She is."

"Jasper?"

"Yeah."

"Why didn't you say anything?"

"I don't know. I didn't want to think about it."

"Okay."

"Did you fuck Ana yet?"

"No."

"Oh."

"I'm starting not to mind."

"Really?"

"Yeah."

"Weird."

"Yeah."

"Let's go back out."

"Okay."

32

I am starting to feel sick. Where is Georgia Treely? I am a very drunk human being. The Georgia Plan. I am not going to be a Dad. 2:35 a.m. I have not seen Tenaya in one or two hours. I decide to look for her.

She is not in the kitchen, the kitchen cupboards, the sofa cushions, the television, or any of the upstairs bedrooms. People are not slumped and sleeping in heaps and on floors yet. People are still drinking and doing sex with each other. The house is still full of loud.

Tenaya is probably outside.

I go to sit in the bathroom. I sit on the toilet seat and stare at my hands. The lines dance. The creases across my fingers spasm.

A sound from across the room.

The boiler cupboard.

I pull open the doors and find Tenaya crouched in amongst the insulation by the boiler. There is just enough space for me to fit in beside her. It feels like we are in a box of jungle air. She has her iPod in. I take the headphone out of her right ear and put it into my left. Bon Iver. Her eyes are estuaries. At least she is not attacking herself.

We do nothing but sit for a while. I know what she is crying about. I feel sentimental. She is crying about Tom but also what Tom is an example of: failure. We all fail often. We fail each other and we fail ourselves. Mum failed Dad, Keith failed Margaret, Tabitha failed Life, Tom failed Tenaya, Jonah failed around thirty girls. I guess I failed Abby. Sorry, Abby.

After half an hour or so, it starts to rain. Water raps at the wall behind our heads as though it has a bladder the size of a coin and we are sat in the only free toilet cubicle. Persistent, steel rain. The sound of rain mismatches the sauna air between us. It is like a girl screaming because she's cut her knee when you're warm in bed reading *Harry Potter*.

When you feel sad, and then it rains, it is called Pathetic Fallacy. Like in *Macbeth*, when Duncan dies and there is a storm. Pathetic Fallacy in real life is like Nature being insensitive. It makes things worse. For this reason, right now, I do not think Mother Nature should be called Mother Nature anymore. It should maybe be called Keith Nature or Tom Nature or Bitch Nature. My glass head has shattered and Tenaya is sad. Mothers do not piss on people when they feel like this, they hug them and curse their enemies.

I pull out my wrap of mephedrone and give us both two corners off of my debit card to make everything better.

I light a cigarette.

Tenaya leans her head against my chest. I can feel the wet from her cheeks seeping into my T-shirt.

"You okay?" I say.

"I don't know." She takes the cigarette out of my hand and draws in from it. "Just feel weird."

"Yeah," I tell her. "I know."

Tenaya lifts up her head. She stares very squarely into my eyes with her eyes. She is trying to climb into my body somehow. She is going to climb in and hide there.

She leans closer and kisses me.

It is a strange thing to be doing, but not too strange because she doesn't look like Tenaya, she looks like a damp blur. I am not thinking about who she is or what she means, I am just thinking about being close to another human body.

We kiss more. She is a confident kisser.

She pushes open the doors of the boiler cupboard. We move out and over to the empty bathtub. She positions her body inside of it. She is a large fetus in a white plastic womb. Her pants are pulled down and off over her lovely left foot.

I shouldn't.

I lay in between her legs. I make simple and enjoyable motions with my pelvis. Her mouth opens. Her head lifts up and smacks against the taps. I do my best.

Afterward I sit up and she lies with her head against my chest. I realize there were small pools of water in the bottom of the bathtub. There are maps of water across the fabric of my trousers. Her hair is wet. Wet like a girl that has drowned in the ocean. A tiny girl. And by accident. And only once.

And there are tears in my eyes because—I don't know why. I can feel my hands quivering. My heart is going fast. Her face is still buried in my chest.

And I realize I have done it.

I have chewed my fingernails until they have bled.

I have hanged myself with a rugby sock.

I have murdered my ex-wife.

At least I'm not going to be a Dad anymore.

I draw myself out from under her and leave the bathroom.

33

I check the time on my phone. 3:11 a.m. I stare at the wall. I check the time on my phone again. 3:12 a.m. There is a half-full can of beer on top of the television, so I take it. I have done three laps of the house and could not find Georgia Treely. My head will not sit still. Nothing will stay in it. A boy and a girl I do not know are huddled together on the sofa. The girl is making small, high-pitched sounds.

Because I do not want to watch people having sex again, I go outside. The air is cold and black. It hurts my throat. There are people asleep in their cars, wrapped in blankets, spooning.

I follow the path hemmed by bushes out through the fields. There is enough light bouncing off the moon to illuminate the path.

I walk for a while then stop. There are sounds coming from behind a section of the bush. There are clothes and shoes at the edge of the path.

I push my head through the bush. Wow. Tom and his new girlfriend are having sex on the grass. They must be very cold. There are goose pimples all over his bare porcelain buttocks.

Pulling my head out of the bush, I unzip my fly. I aim my penis at one of Tom's shoes and shoot neon-yellow piss into it. This makes me feel like justice has been done, sort of. Tenaya would definitely approve.

Where are you, Georgia?

Come to Jasper.

I am an extremely creepy young male.

Further down the path there are more sounds coming from a field on the other side of the bush. They are different kinds of sounds. It sounds like yelping and swearing and mooing. Very intriguing.

I climb through the bush. On the other side of the bush Ping, Jonah and Ana are all naked and running around a group of three cows. Why is everyone getting naked? Ping is holding a large stick and a cow is chasing him. I am laughing.

When Jonah sees me he runs over and encourages me to take off my clothes. I tell him to fuck off. He does not take fuck off for an answer. Jonah and Ana and Ping knock me to the floor and begin pulling off my clothes. I struggle but I'm laughing. I scream that I'm not going to be a

Dad. I wonder what they have taken. Jonah and Ping tug at my trousers and Ana pulls my T-shirt up. Soon I'm on the ground in my boxers with the grass scratching my legs. Jonah's about to try to take them off me but then a large mahogany cow comes running right at us.

I get up and run.

We start running up the field, away from the house.

Jonah stops.

"What?" I say.

He points into the distance. I can vaguely make out a hovering light. I do not have very good eyes. I would not be allowed to become a pilot or a professional hunter.

"It's the fucking farmer," he says. His voice sounds scared but he's grinning.

"Listen," Ping says.

We do.

Barking.

"He's got dogs."

Immediately we all turn on the spot and begin running back toward the cows and the cottage. Cows are far less terrifying than an angry farmer with large dogs.

We run blindly in the opposite direction of the yapping dogs. I pause only to pull my jumper out of a cow's mouth.

I do not stop to look for my other clothes.

I do not stop until I am outside the cottage and can barely breathe.

Ana, Ping and Jonah aren't next to me but I'm not worried for them. I'm sure they got away. I'm sure nobody got eaten. I pull the arms of the jumper over my legs. My boxer shorts slouch down out of the head hole.

Inside the living room of the cottage, I pause.

Georgia Treely.

Time for The Georgia Plan. Look sexy. Look confident.

She is sat alone on the sofa, holding her head. Her hair is full of bright clips and slides. It looks like a nest of fireflies. I want to wear her fireflies across my shoulders. I want permission to touch her skin and squeeze her hard and not think about Keith or Tenaya or Tabitha Mowai or Abby Hall for just a few minutes. I stare at her feet and say nothing. The bones in her feet catch shadows from the light of the dull ceiling lamp. The second *Jackass* film is playing on the television.

For courage, I pick up a half-empty beer can off the floor and down it. Doing this is called "Dutch courage." That is offensive to Dutch people because it implies that they cannot do anything without drinking first.

"Hello, Georgia Treely," I say, standing directly in front of her.

"Oh, Jasper. Hi." She looks me up and down. "Jasper," she says, "why are you wearing a jumper on your legs?"

"No reason," I say. I sit down next to her. "Are you okay?"

"Yes. No. I don't know. I feel a bit ill. I think I drank too much. I don't usually drink."

"Oh," I say. "I'm sorry."

I put my hand on her back and move it up and down. I am showing sympathy. Sympathy is seductive.

"Do you want something to make you feel better?"

"Not drugs, I don't take drugs."

"Not drugs, no. Well, sort of drugs, yes, but legal drugs. So, like coffee really."

"My mum drinks coffee."

"Great. Come on, let's go upstairs for coffee."

I take her hand and lead her upstairs.

Upstairs, in the guest bedroom, me and Georgia Treely have rather large coffees. I assure her that people always have coffees this large.

Georgia Treely stares at the wall for a while. I imagine her head must be fizzing, because this is her first time taking anything.

I tell her that I stare at her in Psychology and that I tried to talk to her on Facebook chat but she wasn't there. She nods at me. She touches my hand. This is the first time she has done drugs. She is going to think she is in love with me.

"I love you, Jasper," she says.

Is this okay? It seems a bit bad. Slightly unethical. Slightly rapey, maybe.

I conduct a very brief moral trial in my head. I use the characters from *Animal Farm.*

> Pig: I strongly object. This is hideous. Doing this would be like pissing into a bone china Ming-dynasty vase.

Dog: Objection, you are victimizing the defendant.

Pig: Objection, only a victim can be victimized.

Rat: Grammatical confuzzlement!

Judge: Irrelevant.

Cow: What is?

Dog: She is pretty fit.

Pig: Very fit, actually.

Judge: Then go for it.

Jasper J. Wolf: Thanks, everyone.

"I love you, too," I say.

I stand up and go over to the bed. The passed-out girl is still on it. I lift her up and lay her on the floor. Georgia Treely lies on the bed. I lie on Georgia Treely. I want a nuclear holocaust to leave nothing but me and Georgia Treely intact.

I think it is probably obvious what comes next and how superbly lovely it feels.

34

7:23 a.m. My head is warm and aching. The room is filled with weak light and the air is heavy like glass. I turn to my left. Georgia Treely's head is next to my head. It looks like the nicest head in the world. She looks a bit dead. I hope she isn't dead. I wonder if this is a joke. If someone has put a fake Georgia Treely head in bed next to me so that I wake up and feel very happy until I try to kiss it and realize that it's plastic. I poke the head. It isn't plastic. I drop a kiss onto her forehead.

Some women only look beautiful to certain men at certain times of the morning in certain light. Georgia Treely is not one of them.

Then I remember what happened last night.

It looks like I may have raped her. I mean she wanted

to but she probably didn't want to want to. It was the drugs that made her want to. In court, I'll say I had no idea. In court, I'll cry until they let me go.

I slide out of the bed. I feel very dizzy. Someone has left their clothes on the floor. I pull them on and quickly leave the room. I am escaping from the scene of the crime.

A girl sprints past the doorway as I am leaving. She disappears down the staircase and out of the house. Her face is the face of someone who has narrowly escaped death. Jonah emerges slowly from the room with a duvet held around his shoulders.

"What the fuck was that?" I say.

Jonah waves an empty packet near my face.

Catholic condom.

I laugh, hard.

"It seemed funny," he says. "I don't know."

"Funny doesn't last that long," I say. "A baby lasts for ages."

"I know. It was stupid." He presses his hands against his eye sockets. "I'm going to sleep now. Night, Jasper."

"Night night."

He throws up the duvet so it covers his face and he stumbles back into the bedroom.

There are people asleep in the hallways and on the stairs and on the floor downstairs. Two boys from Baccant High are still awake and smoking a joint in the kitchen. One of them nods at me. I go to sit outside.

The sky is wide and white, with a wash of early morning mint green. Pink clouds push together and mate. They move in slow teams across the edge of the fields. Everything is very quiet. The quietest quiets always fall after the loudest louds. This is because the quiet can put its arm around you and gesture at the loudness right behind it and say, "Look at that thing compared to me."

I walk round to the side of the house and find Tenaya sat cross-legged on the bonnet of Ping's car. She is smoking and cradling a cup of tea. I climb up next to her.

"Morning," she says.

"Yeah," I say. She passes me the teacup and I take a sip then pass it back. "Last night was—" is all I manage to say next.

"I know," she says. "We were both scared and sad and drunk. Let's talk about it later."

She smiles at me.

"Everything's fine," she says.

"Yeah."

"So what happened afterward?"

I gulp. "Um," I say. "Nothing."

"Go on."

"Fine." Tenaya is always able to make me admit everything. "I think I may have raped Georgia Treely."

Tenaya laughs. "I don't think you raped anyone, Jasper."

"Well, I gave her lots of drugs, then had sex with her."

Tenaya laughs again. "That sounds like most of the sex most teenage girls ever have."

"I'm not sure, it seems bad."

"Don't be stupid." Tenaya finishes the rest of the tea in one long swallow. "Now can we go find Ping and get out of here?" she says.

"Yeah," I tell her. "I'm fucking starving."

We wander around the house a while before finding Ping and Ana asleep in a large cupboard full of socks. We wake Ping for a lift home because neither of us wants to do the walk back to Jonah's car. Ping swears a while when we shake him awake but he realizes that he's hungry, too, and agrees to take us back.

The café Ping drives us to is a plastic, kitcheny type of place, with stained mauve tabletops and badly laminated menus. The waitresses are all foreign. They talk in hurried landslides of hard letters. It is sexy when pretty girls speak ugly languages.

"I'll have the Earlybird Breakfast, please," I say to the waitress.

"Ze vat?"

"Uh, the Earlybird Breakfast?"

"Vat?"

"UHR-LEE-BURD."

I hook my lips around the words as though I'm giving head.

"EH? I no undersan'."

It's not so sexy anymore.

I flap my arms like wings then gesture with my hands toward my mouth. She smiles. Jonah and Tenaya laugh. In the end, I point it out on the menu.

We eat quickly and in silence. When Ping drops me off outside my house, I am only thinking about sleep. Mum isn't thinking about sleep. Mum is stood in the doorway with her hands on her hips.

35

The police interrogation room in which I am sat smells of old wood and coffee. It smells like a room that people do not like to go into. Even the paint on the walls is trying to leave. I want to leave.

"I want to leave," I say. "I'm really tired."

Opposite me is a man who says his name is PC Holloway. PC Holloway has a very faint mustache and large blue eyes. His hands are clasping each other on the table. He is looking at me. The look he is giving me is a neutral one. I am having trouble reading his body language.

"You need to understand that this was a serious waste of police time," he says.

He is talking about Keith. About how Keith isn't really

a murderer and I got it wrong because sometimes I think too much and too hard and for too long. A way of explaining it might be to say that my imagination is a fast-running river and my body is a boat in the river and the boat is just being carried by the current but it has to learn not to. My head hurts.

"I understand," I say. "And I am very, very sorry."

He stands up. I stand up.

"Sit back down," he says.

I sit back down.

"Only joking," he says.

PC Holloway has a very good sense of humor. Some of the funniest people in the world are men. His wife is a very lucky woman.

He leads me to the police station doors and ruffles my hair.

"Be good," he says.

I wish PC Holloway were Mum's husband.

I find Mum sat on the steps leading up to the police station doors. She is smoking a cigarette. I sit down next to her.

"Mum?" I say.

"Yes, Jasper."

"Cigarettes contain tar, which will make your lungs turn black and eat themselves," I inform her.

"Yes, Jasper," she says, crushing out the cigarette. "Thank you."

"You shouldn't take up smoking again. I know you are stressed but cancer is more stressful, I expect."

"I know."

"Okay," I say, standing up. "Can we go home now?"

"Yes, we can."

Mum is angry at me for getting her husband arrested but she still loves me because I am her son.

36

8:30 a.m. I wake up. Radio 4 is still playing. A man and a woman are discussing the future of 3D cinema. I climb out of bed and walk through to the bathroom. In the shower I cough and shiver. My lungs have been ruined by the graffiti of cheap, foreign cigarettes. The water warms. My head clears.

I am very confused.

I feel hollow.

I feel unfulfilled.

But I had sex with Georgia Treely?

Okay.

Georgia Treely is pretty. Georgia Treely is sexually attractive. A court of anthropomorphized animals ruled that I should have sex with Georgia Treely. I had sex with Georgia Treely. Sex is all. Sex is for billboards and magazines. It is not for making major life decisions with. Sex should be a by-product of something else. Georgia Treely is a cow I have killed for leather. You should only kill cows for meat.

What does that even mean? Doesn't matter, at least I'm not going to be a Dad.

I dry my body and dress and go downstairs. Keith is sat at the kitchen table, reading *The Sun*. He looks up.

"Hello," I say.

"Morning."

When we got back from the police station, Keith told me that he had forgiven me. He is a man of exceptional moral fiber. He has, however, stopped using his patronizing friendly names on me. I will have to work hard to regain his trust, so that he calls me "buddy" again.

I pour myself a glass of milk and carry it down to the shed at the end of the garden. I take my notepad out from behind a leaning spade and recommence work on my novel. My novel is almost finished. It is the story of a young man blessed with great charisma and wit, trying to work out what he is supposed to do and how he is supposed to do it. It has everything that I wanted: a sort-of rape scene (sorry again, Georgia), a sort of revelation (sorry again, Keith) and some sort of lesson. I don't know what the lesson is yet, but there is definitely going to be one.

I am Holden Caulfield, only less reckless, and more attractive.

37

3:28 p.m. I am sat with Tenaya in her garden. The sun is huge and close. The chickens are singing. There is a pot of tea between us.

Her mum comes out of the French doors. She is wearing a T-shirt with BOYCOTT ISRAELI GOODS printed on it. She is holding a plate of custard creams.

"Thanks, Mum," Tenaya says. She is as confused as I am.

"Thanks, Mrs. Enright."

"Dad's gone, Ten," her mum says.

"I know."

"He's going to stay with a friend for a while."

"I'm seventeen, Mum. You and Dad are getting a divorce."

Her mum's eyes half close and fill with tears. They burst and tumble down her cheeks.

"I'm sorry," Tenaya says.

She stands up and pulls her mum into a hug. I stand up and hug Tenaya's mum from behind. Her buttocks press against my groin. We are a Tenaya's-mum sandwich. This is not the time for erections. I think of Terry Wogan, naked, doing judo, with Louis Walsh.

After a couple of minutes, she disentangles herself from us. She ruffles my hair.

"You're better off without him, Mrs. Enright," I say.

Tenaya's mum ambles back into her kitchen. We sit back down and watch her taking down pans from hooks on the tiled wall. The smell of frying onions leaks out into the garden.

I put my hand on Tenaya's hand, in a sexy way.

"Jasper," she says, "what are you doing?"

"It's for my novel," I say. "It needs character development and resolution."

"Oh."

"Can I write that we kiss?"

"If you want," she says.

"Okay."

We kiss.